# About th

## James C

James 'the Taxman' Cressey is t.               ....ck Orthodox man and a very unorthodox woman. They met in a betting shop in Stockton, near Newcastle upon Tyne, although they were both from a remote fishing village in France. They made Stockton their home and sold wooden toys to all of the children in the North East. James was supposed to take over the production of these toys, but he couldn't handle such hedonism. Today he works from home for a company that sells accounting software to small businesses.

## Tom Williams

Contrary to popular belief, Tom Williams has never been to space. It's all a lie. He once looked at space from a far distance and decided to tell all his friends that he had been there. He will stand by this lie until the end of his days. Born in 1963, Tom grew up in Basford Green outside Stoke-on-Trent, but hasn't visited Staffordshire this side of the millennium (year 2000). He currently lives with his wife and someone else's two children in a hut at the point where the A34 crosses the A303.

Tom is made of clay.

*Dear Emily Pettman!*
*We love you!*

# SPACE

## It is Set in Space

**By**

**James Cressey**

*or*

**Tom Williams**

**Illustrated by**

**Callum Winter & James Cressey**

Printed on Earth

First Printing, 2018
ISBN 978-1-7314-7463-6
(Intergalactic Space Book Number)

In the unlikely event that any profits are made from this book
they will* be immediately launched into space to help stimulate
the economy of Diligord-5.

Space Publishing Ltd.
Tom or James' House
London
Earth
Nowhere near the Tralmodian System
Space
SP43 E11

*might

*For Sir Dave Benson Phillips*

# Prologue

In a dark part of space, right in the corner by some old forgotten moons without planets and a couple of mouldy, out of date nebulae, an absolutely massive spaceship was floating. It was huge. Bigger than anything that you or I have ever seen. It was an obscenely big spaceship. If you were to walk the full length of this ship, you would be walking for flipping ages.

It was bigger than your average planet, considering mean, mode *and* median. It was so huge, that to see the whole thing with the naked eye meant being really far away from it. To get to this distance, you'd have to travel through space for hundreds of years, by which point you and your naked eye would be dead. If you haven't yet fully comprehended how incomprehensibly big this ship is, I (or we) urge you to reread this opening a few more times.

Further to its ridiculous size, this spaceship was also chock-a-block full of aliens. Proper aliens. Green slimy ones with eight eyes and tentacles.

Algan woke up with a start. Algan was a type of alien called a jotaj, and something was not right with his jotaj body. His left sucker was perked up. His left sucker was *never* normally perked up. It always hung down casually like a wet phonarck's nasal juice valves, the way it should. But this morning it was *well* perked up. Algan panicked and thought to himself *I better see the ship's medic almost immediately.*

One problem with being on a very large ship, and I mean massive (see paragraph one), is that it can take a very long time to get anywhere, especially when your left sucker is all perked up and you obviously can't use the transportation tubes (for hygiene reasons and lowgiene considerations).

It took Algan absolutely ages to to get to the medical sector. The spaceship was really big (if you had forgotten) and for Algan, right now it felt even bigger. He did not need this today. Today was the day of his big test. He was to become a 'Level-4 Hatch Monitor', and today he was being tested on how to manage translucent and bio-bacterial ingest hatches. He had been studying for this test for weeks, and during the last few days he had been as nervous as his mother had been on the day that Algan was born (which is understandable, as jotaj mothers commonly die in childbirth, a fact which results in the common mistake of people thinking that jotaj mothers hate their children and simply can't stand to be around them. Not true. If you see a young jotaj without its mother, it's most likely the mother is dead, or perhaps just not there at the time you are looking at them). It would make perfect sense to think that it was these nerves that led to Algan's left sucker to be all perked up. Wrong! The real reason was much more important and/ or nefarious.

While using the doctor's waiting room for its intended purpose, Algan stared out of the window, thinking about how he was going to take his 'Hatch Monitor Level-4' test if his left sucker was either still sticking up, or in a *cast*! Embarrassing!

A nurse walked in, whose suckers were completely fine, more than fine, but Algan didn't notice this. He was distracted. He saw something far away in the deep blackness of space. It looked like a small spaceship, but this was just perspective. Even though it was impossible for his eyes to be able to focus on something so far away (despite the fact that the eyes of a jotaj are orders of magnitude better than those of a human), he felt as if someone, or something, was looking straight at him and his left sucker.

Instantly, the spaceship was blown apart by this even bigger spaceship with an orange laser. This one was at least three and a half times larger than the first one. *Really* massive. Algan's left sucker was now the least of his problems, as his body was occupying a much, much larger area of space than was possible for someone who was still alive. He, and everything that was on the really big ship we started off talking about, had been obliterated. This left just one question remaining. Why, and for what reason, had this happened?

*Well that sucks!*

# Chapter One:

# The Saddest Golplorx

A small space orb floated in front of him, whistling at a whisper's intensity. The orb was about the size of a pea and glowed a deep purple hue which became orange at its edges. It let off an incredibly faint smell that he'd smelt before, but couldn't quite pin down. This orb was known as a golplorx, and they were a real nuisance.

They were harmless creatures really, get one or two little ones on your skin, or in your gills, and you could get an over-the-counter cream to reduce the swelling, but if you got yourself an infestation then that's when the real problems started. You see, the golplorx had figured out that they were stronger when they worked as a team, and they had created some pretty effective methods of invasion over the years.

By far the most effective method of invasion was introducing a loving, married golplorx couple into the ventilation of a foreign ship and having them reproduce until they could form a reasonably-sized child army. I say married because the golplorx are very old fashioned, and wouldn't even hold hands until the fourth date.

When a child golplorx army is large enough, they then would begin to spread through the ventilation systems of the ship, and slowly engulf each crew member until they are nothing but vapour. Eventually the whole crew would have evaporated, and the golplorx would have themselves a new ship. The only problem then is that they are too small to fly it, but the kick they get out of the exercise is well worth it.

So, while he only had one of these small, purple orbs hovering in front of his face, Horace turned ghost white. For you see, Horace was the ship's ventilation technician, and he knew a young golplorx when he saw one.

\*\*\*

Captain Morf was a great seal of a man – wet, grey skin, a great big belly and whiskers. Horace rushed into his quarters, interrupting his morning snack of six Babybel jammed on to a skewer. This irritated the Captain.

'What the *heck* is going on?! You look like you've seen a ghost!' roared the Captain, using a phrase that is very rarely used when someone has actually seen a ghost. Horace hadn't seen a ghost. He'd seen a golplorx.

Horace didn't quite know how to break the news to the Captain. This was Morf's first voyage back after his suspension, and he didn't have excellent self-esteem at the best of times. Knowing he'd allowed his ship to be overrun by golplorx was going to get him *really* down.

'Spit it out, Horace!'

But before Horace could spit anything out, a humongous

crash echoed from the ceiling of the room.

'It's golplorx, sir! We've been overrun by golplorx!'

'But we have state of the art golplorx detection systems in every vent!'

'Well sir, they were state of the art twenty years ago, but they're still running on Windows 95. I've been telling you we need to upgrade them in every meeting we've had for the last ten years, as well as your superiors during your period of suspension. Golplorx are very adaptive and good at reacting to change, which is why it's so important to keep our systems up to date. I said this would happen!'

The Captain let out a sigh.

'You're right Horace, nobody could have predicted our systems would fail. It's nobody's fault.'

Horace tried to interject, but was interrupted by a shrill voice echoing out from the computer on the Captain's desk.

'It looks like you've been overrun by golplorx! Would you like me to destroy them?'

The golplorx detection system may have failed, but the Captain had also failed to upgrade his personal computer from Windows 95 (intergalactic edition). In a stroke of space-luck, Clippy from Microsoft Office just happened to have a golplorx eradication feature built in.

'Go ahead, Clippy,' Horace grumbled.

And with that, a huge fireball made its way through the

ventilation system, killing every last golplorx dead. Clippy had *finally* been useful. Or so they thought.

\*\*\*

Martin S. Ronson was a golplorx, yes, but he had no interest in killing. He was the most intelligent golplorx to ever have lived, so, obviously, also the saddest. While his friends were screaming *Kill! Kill Kill!*, he was muttering under his breath phrases like *man quantum physics is so interesting, look how the mere act of measurement changes the outcome of reality*, but nobody wanted to hear it. He had always felt unlike the rest of his species, like there was something different in his genes. He had been feeling at his very lowest when he left the vent just before the war plan had been put into action, moments before everybody else had been engulfed by Clippy's fireball.

In fact, it was the presence of Martin S. Ronson that alerted Horace to the golplorx. So, ironically for this pacifist, he unwittingly caused the greatest number of casualties in the history of his species. Martin S. Ronson knew this, and for some reason it made him feel happier than he'd ever felt before. His mother and father had been pretty nice all things considered, but they were really just two normal golplorx, hell-bent on infecting air vents the galaxy over. Martin S.

Ronson dreamt of bigger and better things, and perhaps this would be his only chance to grab them with his tiny floating orb-hands.

He was finally free. He no longer had to endure being a mindless, floating, killing orb. He would be able to fly around the world thinking about quantum physics, and try to make friends with other small spherical aliens who enjoyed pondering these things. Martin S. Ronson now had one sole desire: he would find his calling and he would live his life to the full, he would be a help to those smaller than him, and a friend to those bigger. He would single handedly, which is extremely difficult for a floating orb, enlighten the world as to how nice and courteous a golplorx could be.

With this thought in mind, he flew as fast as he could to the great ship's escape pod control room. He reached it in an acceptable amount of time and with a flourish, Martin S. Ronson set the Windows 95 system to 'eject' and hit 'run'. A floppy disk ejected, which wasn't what he had intended, but he chucked the disk into the hatch all the same and floated in after it.

Back in the Captain's quarters (all five of them, he was a large beast), Captain Morf and Horace were revelling in the destruction of the golplorx army.

'You know Harold,'

'Err, it's Horace, sir,' replied Horace.

'Yes... well, I'm very pleased with how I handled that situation. It was very Captainly of me.'

Horace nodded.

'Here, have a Babybel,' the captain continued. 'I could never have done it without the help of Clippy over here.' Clippy was doing one of those little animations he does when you're not using him. Horace was very mild mannered and did not like to blow his own figurative trumpet, so he just took a bite of the Babybel the Captain had given him. This was the single nicest thing the Captain had ever done for anyone who wasn't directly related to him.

\*\*\*

Horace's utilitarian trouser knee pocket began to vibrate. He ripped open the velcro and pulled out the futuristic tablet he used to monitor the ship. For some ridiculous sci-fi reason the screen was transparent. Horace had an auto-message to say that one of the escape pods had been accessed without authorisation. Horace was responsible for the escape pods as well as the air vents. He quickly flicked over to the corresponding camera. It was the same golplorx from before, flinging something into an escape pod and jumping in after it. Horace's fingers hovered over the lock button, which would securely shut off the operations from the escape hatch and trap the golporx in it. However, at this moment, Horace had a sudden change of heart. He realised that this golporx was a mere child, raised to do one thing, and one thing only (taking over spaceships and killing their crew, to recap, if you're slow). Yet here he was, jumping into an escape hatch, showing no sign of wanting to take the ship through infestation.

'What is it, boy?' huffed Captain Morf.

'Nothing, Captain,' replied Horace, swallowing a lie as well as his remaining Babybel, 'I was just being alerted to the thousands of dead golplorx in the air vents.'

'Very well', replied the Captain. 'Enough chit-chat, you better go and clean up your mess!'

Horace exited the Captain's quarters and took another look at the video stream on the tablet. He could see the golplorx in the pod.

'Space-speed little golplorx, I wish you all the best.' he whispered.

***

The pod released at a terrific speed with Martin S. Ronson safely aboard. It was the kind of speed which looks really slow and quiet when you are far away in space, but something about the way it moves tells you that it's actually at an outstanding velocity. The way a comet slowly glides through the air, or a Formula One car swerves around a corner, all part of the harmony that keeps this Universe in check.

Martin S. Ronson was out, he was gone, he had left the ship where he had been born, but the reality was that today he was starting his life. You may, for some reason, think that his part in this saga was over, but you would be sorely mistaken, so sorely mistaken you'd need to Savlon and plaster up your mistake. For Martin S. Ronson had a floppy disk.

Martin S. Ronson had *the* floppy disk.

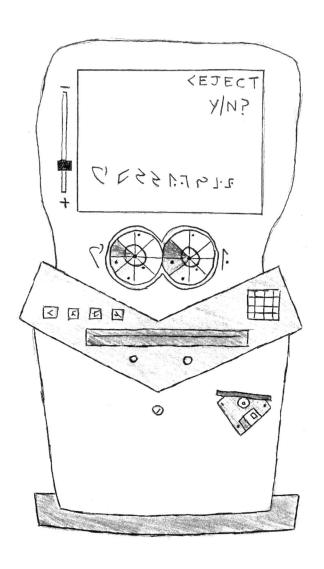

*A Fatal Error?*

# Chapter II

There is a planet not far from space that has found itself in a right economical pickle. Due to a spelling mistake in the constitution of Diligord-4, you are able to use whatever currency you like to pay for goods and services. Prices are simply presented as a number, and you can pay in whatever currency you have in your dirty, little, tartan-lined space-pockets. It is not hard to see what an issue this is when you are trying to run a business on Diligord-4. However, it does mean the number of bank heists are dramatically low.

Eraow stood behind his shop counter. Eraow sold yoffa. He sold yoffa by the kilo and he got a lot of attention for it. The store was called *However You Pay, It's All Okay*. It was a kind of store/café called a Nocobot store, selling all kinds of nick nacks, and a few stale bags of actual Nik Naks. It's a little known fact that Nik Naks are a space delicacy, loved all over the universe for their odd shapes and tangy taste. In the early '60s a bag of Nik Naks fell to Earth, and the Tories attempted a huge cover up to stop people asking too many questions on how Nik Naks came to be. The cover up was *almost* a complete success, in that Nik Naks can now only be purchased at swimming pool vending machines in the UK.

A young jeren came into the store and asked Eraow how much it would cost him for 2.34 kilos of yoffa.

'It's 12 for that much,' Eraow replied, scratching his

bald, slimy, pulsating, chin valve.

'For 2.34 kilos of yoffa? You gotta be kidding me!' Reluctantly the jeren handed over twelve ekcles. He took the bag of yoffa, put it in his glaretram sack, popped on his surogou space-gloves, for it was cold outside, and made to walk out the Nocobot store. All the while, there had been an oleald sitting at one of the tables, pouring her yoffa into her foul yimello tract. She piped up.

'12 eckles? 12 eckles?! I just payed 12 resaix for 1.89 kilos of this, *quite honestly*, substandard yoffa! One resiax is worth a whole lot more than one eckle!'

'Look here,' replied Eraow, 'When you come to Diligord-4 you have to learn to pay how the locals pay. It costs 12, and 12 is what it costs. If you want to go to some other planet with its fancy economies and currencies and stock markets and exchange rates then go there, but *here* you pay *12*.' Eraow tilted his titlilating toob, and turned away from the oleald.

'I've lived on this planet for years, I know about the economy, and I know about how it's exploited by people like you!'

Eraow turned back to the oleald.

'Diligord-4 years?' he asked.

'YES DILIGORD-4 YEARS, YOU IMBECILE! Why would I be using any other planet's timing systems?!'

'...and what do you mean *people like you*?' said Eraow.

'I mean,' seethed the oleald, 'Fat, dirty spleehae nazes!'

She was getting really riled up now. The oleald was well built, with broad shoulders that looked like they could hug you right up (she didn't hug that often though). Her face was firm and squishy in all the right places, to the right person she was beautiful, but to the wrong person she was incredibly offensive. You never knew who you were until you saw her.

'What was the point of the intergalactic-federal-cosmic-government-space-agency making contact and taking over this planet sixty-five years ago if you don't use Diligord-4 years?! Next thing you'll be telling me that the town hall is only 1.5 miles away!'

Her face was going very green now. Green, as you know, is the colour olealds go when they get angry, because on their home planet blue, pink and grey are the primary colours *[editor's note: check this]*. Also, the town hall was exactly 1.5 miles away.

'THIS PLANET IS JUST CHOCK FULL OF ABSOLUTE JIMMAJABBERS!' she shouted.

Eraow almost fell back in shock. This was just far too much for a Sunday afternoon (and it wasn't even a Sunday).

'GERRRR'OUT OF MY SHOP!' he roared out of his larger ming-hatch, his two reverse tentacles flailing wildly above him.

With a look of thunder, the oleald stormed out of the store, and made her way down the street to get the next ship back to her home planet with its strong economy and credit cards, breaking the one rule her father had sworn her to live by. As she walked down the street she looked at the shop windows. She saw all sorts for sale; yboiveths, strethnoids, bingjaks, nemowyxes, toojits, flizzhammers, neilaekaf and nekmids. All with prices next to them. Numbers, numbers which could be paid for with any kind of currency you had in your pocket.

This backward, inverted, crazy planet was really starting to get on her nerves. She had spent thousands of resiax in the god-forsaken years she had been stationed here. She could have spent thousands of eckles, or thousands of toximbles, even. This enraged her. It really, really annoyed her. She was so seriously, actually miffed about it, and this planet should know by now, after everything that it and its government had been through in the past sixteen years, that it was *never* a good idea to tick off the daughter of the king! That's right, the king!

*However You Pay, It's All Okay*

# The Third
# Chapter

The feeling of freedom was starting to wear off. Martin S. Ronson had been in the escape pod for over four days. Four days is a long time for anyone to be stuck in a small enclosed space, even in space where there are no clocks (I realise that two meanings of the word 'space' are used here in the same sentence. Isn't the English language peculiar?). Luckily, Martin S. Ronson is very small, so it could have been a lot worse, space-wise. He was bored, however.

Unfortunately, the floppy disk that he had taken from Captain Morf's ship was incompatible with the escape pod's computer, and all he could do to pass the hours was wonder what was on it, and why it had fallen into his figurative hands. He tried staring at it for a long period of time, hoping to see the 1s and 0s in its core. He tried smelling it and even licking it, but to no avail.

If you've never found yourself stuck inside an escape pod which is hurtling through space at a really high speed, or been kept in solitary confinement for crimes which you won't be asked about, or had to endure the mind-numbing ramblings of the Rambling Mind-Numbers from Centigal-Vox, then you most likely don't know what it's like. It's boring.

Martin S. Ronson had tried all sorts to keep himself entertained. He'd looked out the window at the view which was big and black and empty, he'd played Minesweeper on the onboard computer for a while until he remembered it was a really dull game (and the celebration animation on the little yellow face when you win really wasn't worth the effort), he had even gone so far as to systematically and alphabetically name all of the 126 characters from his favourite TV show, *Mothers of Tsars Dance with the Stars*. He'd even come up with own business idea, *Milk by Celebrities*. Effectively you get celebrities to milk some space-cows and slap a huge price label on it. People will pay for anything done by celebrities. Alas, for Martin S. Ronson, not even these game changing business opportunities were resolving his boredom.

This budding intergalactic adventurer was starting to form a plan, and top of his list of things to do to improve his life was to get a body to transform him from a little orb to a hot, bipedal creature. He felt that without this he may find it hard to move from budding intergalactic adventurer to a full-blown adventurer like Indiana-Galactic Jones *[Editor's note: was this a pun on intergalactic? I don't think it works]*.

You may not know, or you may be able to hazard a guess, but it's quite hard to just get on and do things when you are a golplorx, let alone be taken seriously. When your whole existence is to be a small, floating orb with a deep purple hue that was slightly orange around the edges and gave off a faint smell of something that might be going off in the fridge, but it's not quite intense enough to work out what exactly it is, so you remove every item one at a time gently sniffing to see if it's that particular item until the fridge is completely empty and smells fine so you put everything else back in, well, if that were your existence, you would find it rather difficult to become an intergalactic explorer too.

The question was simple. How was he going to *find* this new body? The answer is simple too, really. With enough money, anything is possible in space.

In space, if you have enough money, you can pay to have dark matter inserted directly into your primary sensory valve, whether that be a seilui, an eye, a beak bladder or an anus. You can buy one thousand beautiful robots with large organs, and have them explode upon your command. In fact, for double that price, you can have two thousand beautiful robots with large organs explode on your command.

With enough money you can even buy an HD DVD (which is different to Blu-Ray, the format that won the high-definition optical-disk format war of the early 2000s) of *Shrek the Third*, and have it converted to Betamax. You must get the picture, with enough money you can pay for anything in space.

If he arrived at a planet whose currency was worth less than his own, Martin S. Ronson was confident that he could get a body. A nice, big, functioning body, that would prove very practical in his bid to live his life to the full. Unfortunately, his currency was almost worthless... so, it was lucky then, that his escape pod was heading straight toward that economic jewel of space that was Diligord-4.

Martin S. Ronson started dreaming about his life with a lovely, functioning body. He dreamt about the kind of body he would have. He dreamt about muscular bodies with three eyes and large nipples like on the adverts. He dreamt about a body so streamlined that people who tried to pick him up would drop him straight away, even though he was not slippery at all. He also dreamt about a body that was really good looking, but existed only in the second dimension, meaning if he turned to his side he would disappear.

It was this 'turning to the side and disappearing' that awoke Martin S. Ronson from his daydream. His awakening was quickened by the fact that his escape pod was entering the atmosphere of Diligord-4. It was tumbling and burning and rumbling at an incredibly distressing level. The whole pod was vibrating intensely, so intensely that at one point, for a whole two seconds, the vibrations formed a perfect resemblance to the opening notes of Madonna's 1983 hit 'Lucky Star'. Martin S. Ronson didn't even have time to think how weird this was, as he was being flung left, right and centre, and left again, like a sentient bowling ball on a dance mat.

A large parachute shot out of the back of the pod, and was filled with Diligord-4 air. A sudden snap reduction in falling speed inflicted a very minor whiplash on Martin S. Ronson, but nonetheless he would try to claim some form of compensation from his space-insurance eventually. To his great relief, his descent smoothed, and he gracefully made his way down towards the planet's surface.

\*\*\*

A consequence of space being so flipping big is that it is very common for large coincidences to form. Just think about the number of coincidences that you may experience going about your day:

*Oh what a coincidence, that you are in this cinema and so am I!*

*Oh what a coincidence, that you like chocolate oranges and so do I!*

*Oh what a coincidence, that you are wearing the same dress as her!*

This last one wasn't much of a coincidence, but more to do with the fact that there was only one dress and two people, so they had to share.

The coincidence here was not one that Martin S. Ronson

or anyone nearby was aware of, but it still counts. The parachute was one of those novelty chutes that you get, you know the ones. The acquisitions manager on Captain Morf's ship had been a right joker. He had decided to have his face printed on the parachute. It is believed that a similar thing had happened on the Titanic. In both instances, this was a result of the acquisitions manager thinking that they would never actually need to use the escape pod or parachute (in defense of the one on the Titanic, no one did use a parachute in the end).

However, unlike the acquisitions manager of the Titanic, the acquisitions manager of Captain Morf's ship just so happened to look identical to the presenter of hit '90s children's television show *Get Your Own Back*, Sir Dave Benson Phillips. So, Martin S. Ronson, who was no longer being flung all over the place, braced for impact as he floated through the sky in his escape pod, supported by a massive parachute with Sir Dave Benson Phillips' face on it. If we ever make this book into a film, which I am sure we will, we have been assured that Sir Dave Benson Phillips has a reasonable day rate.

The impact was short but sweet. It was short because it only took a few moments, and it was sweet because landing on an alien planet is really badass. Martin S. Ronson slammed the big blue button labelled 'Open Air Hatch'. The air hatch opened. The golplorx breathed in his first breath of Diligord-4 air and floated out onto the planet. He was bloody lucky that all golplorx children are legally required to be immunised. Common sense is popular amongst golplorx parents.

Despite being born on Captain Morf's ship, Martin S. Ronson had of course seen other planets on television. However, even the power of television had not prepared him for the wonders he was encountering on his first day here. There were snorkleflarts and rumpleblacks trailing the streets for food, there were fantislers and rabbits wandering around looking for love. There was a handsome man attempting to sell a marrow to a pretty girl. There were ludicrously named aliens on every street of the city and Martin S. Ronson was loving it. His little orb-like eyes were well and truly boggling.

Whilst floating down the street, he saw from afar a rather disgruntled looking female oleald pacing towards him. Being a polite golplorx, Martin S. Ronson floated to one side. This wasn't enough, however, and as she passed she muttered a curse word under her breath and batted him away. This wasn't the start that Martin S. Ronson had been hoping for, and it wasn't the last time he would have an interaction with the daughter of the king (and it wasn't the second).

After recovering from a mild concussion, Martin S. Ronson floated back into the air to find a Bodyshop. You may know the Bodyshop as an extremely pungent store, that sells a variety of useless items that have been disguised as useful ones. In an amazing twist of fate, the stench of the Bodyshop that you know and love is identical to the faecal matter of a golplorx.

Martin S. Ronson was not aware of this as he floated towards the space-Bodyshop on Diligord-4, nor would he ever become aware of this during his part in this story, and I for one see that as a terrible shame, as it could have made him his fortune.

The Bodyshop in question had a smaller sign above the main sign, and it became apparent that it was in fact known as *Biffin Bambright's Bodacious Bodyshop*. It was located on a street called Hamsmithe Street in a building that was three stories high. That meant it had three separate floors. It does not mean, as is the colloquial term, that it was a three-mouthed lizard-like creature which had smoked so much space-whizz that it was telling three stories at once.

The shop was sandwiched between an 'Underwater Nourishment Store' and a shop that sold DVDs, including an HD DVD of *Shrek the Third*. Martin S. Ronson pondered this for a moment, and then entered the Bodyshop.

'Good afternoon,' stated the gentleman behind the

desk, without looking up from his copy of *Far From the Intergalactic Madding Crowd,* 'and welcome to Biffin Bambright's Bodacious Bodyshop. I am the aforementioned Biffin Bambright. How can I help you today?'

With this, Biffin lifted up his large cylindrical head, only to find that he could not see that any customer had entered the door.

'Hmm. It must have been the wind,' muttered Biffin to himself in the kind of way that real people don't.

'Excuse me,' chirped Martin S. Ronson, 'I am, in fact, here. I'm just a small floating orb known as a golplorx.'

'A golplorx! In my shop! Why, I had my air filters cleaned out just last week! I had better go and get my portable vacuum cleaner.' Neither Hoover or Dyson were household names in this part of space, and therefore everyone used the correct term 'vacuum cleaner'. The same could not be said for Jacuzzi, Rollerblades and Tupperware, unfortunately.

'Wait!'

Martin S. Ronson had to think quickly, lest he be vacuumed up, prematurely ending our story or giving us that now overused plot twist where the main character dies at the start of the book and you're like, 'Woah, I didn't see that coming! What a load of wasted character development!', and then, I don't know, I guess we'd make the guy from the Bodyshop the main character because we're in his shop now. Martin S. Ronson did not want the story to go down this path and neither do we, nor do you. Fortunately for Martin S. Ronson, he saw something on the wall that he recognised.

'Excuse me, is that a poster of Maria Feodorovna and Bradley Walsh, winners of season nine of *Mothers of Tsars Dance with the Stars*?'

He anxiously waited for Biffin Bambright to respond. He did.

'No, you absolute moron! There have only been seven seasons of *Mothers of Tsars Dance with the Stars*! Maria Feodorovna has never appeared on the show with Bradley Walsh. Are you a complete thicko or what?!'

'I'm sorry Mr Bambright…'

'I prefer Mrs Bambright.'

'I'm sorry Mrs Bambright, you see, the golplorx are a little different to the other galactic races in that we experience all of time in one instant. I have seen all of the series simultaneously. Fortunately, the quality of the show never declines.'

'Oh,' replied a puzzled Mrs Bambright, 'but if you don't mind me saying, you appear to be nervous at the possibility that I am going to vacuum clean you. Why are you nervous if you already know the outcome of this conversation?'

Martin S. Ronson was incredibly nervous. He didn't

experience all of time in one instant, he always got his nines and sevens confused, and had mixed up Bradley Walsh with Louis Walsh once again. He was now thinking very quickly on his metaphorical feet.

'It's an evolutionary thing. People are less trusting of people that know all of their past, present and future. I'm not actually nervous. But I wish you no harm. I am a golplorx, yes, but I am a pacifist. I hate how our species have been portrayed in mainstream media. We're not all like that. Some of us read books. Some of us attend to our space gardens. Some of us watch *Hot Tub Time Machine 2* a few times a week and always laugh.'

'It is a hilarious film'.

'Damn straight it is. I know the outcome of this conversation. We become friends. The best of friends. And we have some really cool adventures together, Mrs Bambright'.

'You have convinced me space orb. I'll put the vacuum cleaner away!'

And with that, Mrs Bambright packed away his vacuum cleaner (which actually *was* an imported, branded Hoover) and offered Martin S. Ronson a cup of space-tea. Which is regular tea with condensed milk in it. It's horrible. Martin S. Ronson didn't want a cup of horrible tea, so he got straight down to business.

'Excuse me, do you have a floppy disk drive on these premises?'

Mrs Bambright looked at his new best friend and smiled.

'I'm sorry, we haven't had a floppy disk drive since the plague of millennium bugs swarmed through here and destroyed all forms of pre-Trump storage. We do have a floppy disk to TrumpDrive™ converter though!'

'That sounds useful!'

Martin S. Ronson had his hopes up.

'Unfortunately, my friend, one TrumpDrive™ costs eight hundred. So unless my new friend is extremely wealthy then…'

Mrs Bambright trailed off when he saw what the orb had produced. A floppy disk, and eight hundred golplorx. Yes, the golplorx currency was also called golplorx, and yes, that does get confusing. Fortunately, one golplorx is virtually worthless, so you can only buy half a Twix with that on their planct. And, yes, they do sell Twixes by the half.

You may be wondering where Martin S. Ronson had been keeping his money and the floppy disk this whole time, just being a floating orb. Well, if you would be quiet for a second and allow me to explain, then I will tell you. But if you continue to create such a racket then I couldn't possibly be heard over your obnoxious bellowing. Ask later when you're less drunk.

'Follow me to the TrumpDrive™ room…'

One TrumpDrive™ drive (the storage disk was named a TrumpDrive™ by marketers who didn't understand that the drive was where you insert the disk, so the drive had to be called a TrumpDrive™ drive. It was actually *this* that caused Donald Trump to resign from his presidency) required a whole room as it was so large. Donald Trump had wanted to take America back to the golden age of computing, when computers were massive. With the technology of the day, however, this meant each TrumpDrive™ drive could read petabytes of data in microseconds, and was eventually heralded as a great idea. Take that congress!

Martin S. Ronson wanted so badly to know what was on the floppy disk he had been carrying through space. He inserted it into the floppy disk conversion slot on the TrumpDrive™ drive and waited. The machine made its initial whirring sound. There were no moving parts in a TrumpDrive™ drive, but they added a noise after the first few hundred were returned because people wanted to hear their damn computer doing some damn work.

The two space acquaintances moved around to the output console. They waited as a loading bar got to 99% and then stayed there for a while. They drank some space-tea. Finally, the loading bar disappeared and the contents of the floppy disk were presented. Both space-acquaintances let out an audible gasp.

The screen was blank.

'Oh!' exclaimed Mrs Bambright, 'the floppy disk is in the wrong way round!'

They turned over the floppy disk. Immediately, the TrumpDrive™ drive turned itself off. All of the machines in the shop turned themselves off. And then they all turned themselves on again. Only this time, something about them was gravely, gravely different.

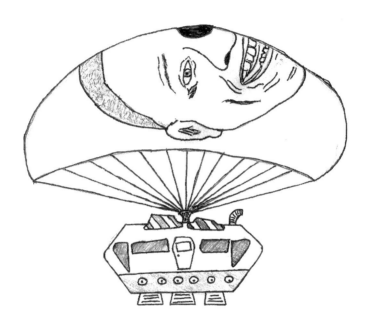

*The gentle descent of Martin S. Ronson*

# -4-

# The Daughter of the King!

Remember the daughter of the king that Martin S. Ronson floated into earlier? Well, you can call her Stardew. Her actual name was something completely different, something that is not only so difficult to pronounce that your speech systems are required to vomit three times in order to get the correct timbre on the first syllable, but it also cannot be typed with a QWERTY keyboard or even the symbols section on Microsoft Word which *does* appear to have any symbol you could wish for. No, she went by the name Stardew because it made life easier. It also sounded badass. You might be thinking that being in space everyone would have got bored of putting *star* in the title of things, but no, it was still cool.

She was still really hacked off. Why was it that she, the daughter of the king, was having to be stationed on this rubbish little planet with its terrible economic systems and golplorx hanging around on street corners? Her father, the king, had sent her away over 16 space-years ago to ensure civil responsibilities were being upheld by the good people of Diligord-4, and to be honest, they often were. Streets were kept clean, bad people were locked up, cigarette butts were viciously thrown back at people who dropped them on the street, and this all resulted in one thing for Stardew – a dull life.

Her life here was *particularly* boring. She went to work

each day and had seen so many TV shows that you could say it was box game, SET, and match for TV. Watching TV all day sounds really fun at first, but it grows tiresome. Some days she would go for a scout around the towns and cities of Diligord-4, looking for some trouble, and when she couldn't find any she would chill out by her pool or play space-croquet. It was a dull, dull life of leisure. Today that was all going to change.

She'd had enough. This yoffa debacle had been the last straw and she was completely cross! Storming through the streets she had but one destination, her office in the Town Hall. She was going to pick up her hoverbike and then drive across the city to her ship, which was parked in one of the most expensive docking stations on Diligord-4.

You may have thought that her plan would have been to rewrite that constitutional error that had resulted in the terrible financial pickle that the planet was in, but no, she was beyond this, and now intended to destroy the whole planet, constitution and all. She knew of course that her father would be furious at this action but *so what*?! He had forsaken her here all that time ago and anyway, he was 0.5 light years away, which was still really far even though it wasn't a whole number.

She entered the town hall, which was, as always, buzzing with a plethora of space creatures that had jobs to be getting on with. If you were to look around you when standing in this hall, you would have been in awe of all the amazing aliens and the creative minds that came up with their design. It would be similar to that scene in the *Harry Potter* series where Harry first enters Diagon Alley and is blown away by all the wizards and magic. He also does this at Hogwarts, the Ministry of Magic, the Quidditch World Cup, Ron's House and Hogsmead. GET OVER IT, HARRY!

Stardew, however, was in no respect blown away. She entered this hall almost daily, and for that reason alone she shot past all the fantastically thought-up alien species and headed straight down corridors, along hallways, and up space-elevators to the reception of her office. Her office was pretty futuristic even for space, everything was very shiny and there were flashing red lights all over the place. Along one wall was what looked like an old 1960's computer system printing out slips of paper with numbers on. These numbers referred to the state of the planet's political and civil situations, but underneath the seven printers were wastepaper baskets which were slowly being filled. Stardew hadn't looked at one of these slips for about 17 months and nothing had really been going wrong. She did shred and recycle every slip though. She used to use the shredded paper as bedding in her hamster's cage. Behind a sci-fi typewriter (the keys are hovering and the paper is see-through) was sitting her trusty, but kind of past-it receptionist Mr Carmichael. He was sipping a cup of tea (regular tea, not space-tea) and playing the incredibly racist game Space Invaders, which people sort of tolerated because he was old. Mr Carmichael was a good looking alien for his age. He always looked dapper, and today he was sporting a navy-blue checkered skinny suit with a matching bowler hat perched on top of his waxle-rump, right at the top of his head, where waxle-rumps are supposed to be.

'Oh, good afternoon Ms Guisher,' Mr Carmichael said slowly, 'I didn't expect you to be coming in today.' Guisher was Stardew's surname and she liked the way Mr Carmichael didn't call her Stardew, as it helped maintain the employee-employer relationship.

'I know Mr Carmichael, but there's been a slight change of plan with my schedule, and I've decided to destroy Diligord-4 immediately!'

'Dear me, Ms Guisher, that's a rather drastic course of action to take on such a sunny afternoon. Wouldn't you rather join me for a game of Space Invaders?' Stardew grimaced at this, it really was sickening that such a game was ever made.

'I'm sorry, Mr Carmichael, but this is just the way it's got to be. I'm completely sick of this whole planet, it really deserves to be destroyed once and for all!' She said this last bit in an Evil Overlord kind of way (with a little bit of a cackle), but Mr Carmichael didn't notice.

'Well, I can only assume that this whole destruction of the planet thing means that the cold hand of death is to finally come knocking at my door? Will I get any form of redundancy package to enjoy in the last few moments of my life? Maybe the rest of the day off to spend with my exceptionally, ridiculously large extended family? Of course you can pay me in any form of currency that you wish!'

The death of Mr Carmichael hadn't really occurred to Stardew until this moment. She had been thinking about the desolation of Diligord-4 as a sphere hanging in the sky, rather than the home of many living souls, one of whom was her trusty receptionist, who was extremely skilled in turning away clients and telling people on the phone that 'Ms Guisher isn't here at the moment,' when she clearly was. No, everyone else on this planet could burn for all she cared, but *not* Mr Carmichael.

'No, Mr Carmichael! There will be no redundancy package for you this day!' Stardew exclaimed, triumphantly. Mr Carmichael looked crestfallen. He had been working for Stardew for 16 years, given the best years of his life for her and her family, and had never taken a sick day in all that time. This is not advisable. If you are genuinely sick you should take a sick day, as you could be contagious and threaten the health of your co-workers by turning up for work. On the other hand, if you wake up feeling a bit groggy don't just take a sick day for the sake of it when you'll probably be feeling fine by 11am, that's taking the piss. 'Don't be sad Mr Carmichael! There will be no redundancy package, because you are coming with me!'

Stardew ran to her office and flipped open the lid which was hiding the big red button. The lid was disguised as a large pile of paperwork so that no one would lift it up to find the button by mistake. This big red button had been designed and installed almost 500 years previously during the great atomic stand-off between the countries of Dalgath and Rispson, over whether the fluff you find inside the pockets of new pairs of jeans could be used as currency on Diligord-4. In the event that it was deemed okay to use this fluff, the owner of the office would press the button, starting a thirty minute countdown to complete annihilation of the planet. This was important because they knew how much jean-pocket-fluff reserves were stored under Dalgath – a vast amount that would destroy the economy of the other 19 major cities on Diligord-4.

The button would arm a massive vaporiser to remove the core of the planet, and cause the rest of the planet to implode in a cataclysm the rest of the galaxy had not seen for millenia. This just goes to show how angry Stardew was on this day. It had been pent up for ages and was now ready to come out.

Firstly, she accessed her emails and switched on her Out of Office. She included a message stating that she no longer worked there. Cleverly and painstakingly, she hid a code where the first letter of each line read out 'UR ALL GON DIE'. By the time the planet was destroyed, nobody had actually read the out of office message, so this act was redundant.

This forms part of a paradox named Schrödinger's Prank, in which someone sets up a prank that they will never see the consequences of. They receive the satisfaction of the prank in the setting up of it rather than when it actually plays out, therefore the reward comes before the result, at which point the prankster does not know, or need to know, whether it will work or not.

A common example is to switch the labels that say 'salt' and 'pepper' in a restaurant. After doing so you may laugh to yourself, thinking about the hilarity of the next customer wanting to use salt and instead using pepper. Following this laugh you might as well return the labels to the correct way and carry on with your day, as you have already enjoyed the satisfaction of a prank well done, without having to actually ruin anybody's meal.

Stardew had never heard of Schrödinger's Prank and probably would have found it tiresome. She looked around her office and, with no real feelings of remorse, she hit the button.

'THIRTY MINUTES!' cried out a pre-recorded voice from long ago. The voice played out across the whole planet, and everyone with fully functioning copular organs stopped what they were doing. They stared up at the sky, breathing what was to be one of their last few hundred breaths, depending on how tired they were and the type of respiratory system they had. They then returned to whatever they were doing in the first place, peeved by what they thought was an obnoxious voice telling them a nearby shop was about to close, or that a space-train was due to leave in half an hour or something similar.

Back in the office, Stardew stared at the button. That was it now, no turning back. She had pressed the button and made the biggest decision of her life. She had changed the course of intergalactic history forever.

'Come, Mr Carmichael! We haven't much time!'

'Only 29 minutes and 48 seconds to be precise,' replied Mr Carmichael.

'Exactly! My hoverbike is in the underground car park. You can ride in the sidecar. To have any chance of leaving this planet alive, we must get to my ship in the posh part of town in about ten minutes. Here, wear these stereotypical racing goggles, you might just need them!'

Her heart was pounding. Finally, some excitement in her life! She didn't know what the next half hour would bring, and she liked it that way. For too long she had endured the monotony of Diligord-4 and from now on it was danger, adventure and uncertainty all the way home!

Down in the car park she revved the engine of the hoverbike, with Mr Carmichael safely seated in the sidecar. He was having a space-whale of a time. Long ago in receptionist school he had been trained for events such as this, but he had forgotten most of his training and was just enjoying every second as it came.

They shot up the ramp of the underground car park, not even bothering to scan their employee badges, and smashed right through the barrier. Time was not on their side! At high speed, Stardew was pulling out all the action-scene maneuvers necessary to make it to her ship before the planet blew. She screeched around a corner and jumped three red lights in a row while *Bat Out of Hell* blasted through her state-of-the-art hoverbike sound system.

Mr Carmichael was shouting out what he believed to be helpful comments to Stardew, such as 'Watch out for the baby!' and 'There's no way you can make that gap!'.

As Meatloaf launched into the second chorus, Mr

Carmichael had a thought. He, of course, knew that *Bat Out of Hell* was 9 minutes and 52 seconds long, and that if the second chorus was already playing, then they must be approaching halfway through the song. He glanced at his watch. They only had 25 minutes left until the planet went up in smoke, which left just 5 minutes to reach the ship! If you are very committed you can actually read this section of the book in time with the second half of *Bat Out of Hell*, so the explosion happens on the last note of the song. This will require a lot of effort and rereading, so I wouldn't bother, if I were you.

At the top of his voice, Mr Carmichael let Stardew know just how little time they had left. They were passing down the back alley of a row of shops, and right at this moment Stardew saw something that took her breath away. She has fantastic vision, as olealds do, and could see directly into the back of a store where two unlikely people were staring at a screen. One was a large, portly creature with a cylindrical head wearing an apron, and the other was a small floating orb. It wasn't just any orb. It was the same golplorx that she had batted aside earlier that day.

She screeched to a halt outside the door and hopped off her bike, much to the surprise and fear of Mr Carmichael, who pointed at his watch. It was not the creatures that had startled her, it was the screen and what it was showing. As has been stated previously, there was no time to lose, but she had to find out what was going on here. She arrived at the door of Biffin Bambright's Bodacious Bodyshop.

'You two! Quickly! This planet is set to explode in 24 minutes time. What the hell is on that screen?!'

Mrs Bambright and Martin S. Ronson turned to Stardew the oleald and then turned to each other, trying to put into words what they had just seen on the screen. Martin S. Ronson began to speak.

'Well… I found a floppy disk… and… well…'

'There's no time to waste!' Stardew screamed. 'Come with me, we're getting out of here! Bring the disk and explain later!'

Mrs Bambright moved towards Martin S. Ronson.

'Blimey,' he whispered, 'that's the daughter of the king! We'd better do as she says. If we're gonna bring the floppy disk, we might as well bring the TrumpDrive™ too!'

With the floppy disk and the TrumpDrive™ in hand (don't worry about the size of the TrumpDrive™), the two acquaintances flew out the door and hopped onto the hoverbike, which was now far too over-subscribed. Stardew hit the accelerator, and the four unlikeliest of heroes sped off to her ship. One thing was for sure, Martin S. Ronson hadn't managed to get a new body, and, as the last whiff of the Bodyshop left his nostrils, he shouted out 'Here we go again!', which didn't make any sense, but he was *stressed.*

*The classic 'Schrödinger's Prank'*

# Part Five

Golplorx don't usually ride bikes, neither pedal-driven nor petrol-fuelled. In fact, Martin S. Ronson was the first to don a tiny, tiny motorcycle helmet (there was one left over from Stardew's recently deceased space-hamster, named Roger) and feel the wind against the front side of his orbular body/face. He was loving it.

Mrs Bambright, however, used to ride in a motorcycle gang, and had killed twice. The first time was an accident, he left his bike unlocked outside a space-Aldi and it rolled down a hill and crushed a toad. The second time was not an accident. The first toad he killed had a large extended family, who were the largest gangster family in the county. They came for him, but as they were toads, were very easy to overpower. Once he had killed the nastiest looking toad (who was named Felix), the rest of the family scarpered.

The king's daughter was a very average hover-cyclist. She had passed her test, but only just. If she wasn't the daughter of the king, then the assessor, who happened to be the cousin of the king, may not have judged her so lightly. But the universe is a nepotistic place, so here she is with a license. To be be fair she probably would have passed eventually, so it's not too much of a bother.

They arrived relatively unscathed to the posh part of town, just as they could hear Meatloaf's vocal cords straining from the previous nine minutes of overwork.

The vocal cords formed a union in 2008, and Meatloaf's performances have never been the same again. The four amigos leapt from the hover bike just as it exploded, as always happens at the end of *Bat Out of Hell*.

'What fortune!' exclaimed Martin S. Ronson.

'That wasn't fortune,' replied Stardew, 'I'm shit hot.'

It was fortune.

\*\*\*

Sometimes when I am asleep I like to think about space, and how big it is and how small that makes me feel. But then I remember what an incredible writer I am, and my ego inflates, and then space starts to look a bit smaller and before long I'm feeling claustrophobic and feel as if the sides of space are pushing up against my cheeks. This is how our four space heroes were currently feeling. The ship was built for two, but only really comfortably held one, like a two-alien tent. There were now three full sized aliens (one of whom was a little overweight), and a small floating orb crammed inside. It was not ideal.

'This isn't ideal,' stated Mrs Bambright.

'Correct,' replied Stardew, 'this ship is only a two-seater, and I just use it to hop from planet-to-planet from time-to-time. Sometimes I use the spare seat to hold my bags or jacket, and sometimes I use it to hold an alien whom I'm on a date with. Anyway, enough of this jibber-jabber, this planet is about to explode. The key is in the back pocket of my jeans, but I can't quite reach it like this!'

It may or may not have been mentioned by this point, but Stardew had an incredible space-arse, supported in a pair of excellent Levi 501s. It would be fair to say that Mrs Bambright had certainly noticed this. He practically jumped (which wasn't anywhere near possible in the cramped space ship conditions) at the opportunity to pull a key out of the back pocket of her jeans.

'I reckon I can reach it if I stretch my central arm out counter-clockwise,' said Mrs Bambright. And so he did.

Weirdly, as he pulled the key (which was of the classic key-shape) out of the back pocket of Stardew's jeans and away from that lovely space-bum, it had a strange kind of blueish goo attached to the bottom, which stringified and dripped as he pulled at it until it snapped, leaving a residual residue on the key. Mrs Bambright decided not to make a scene of this scene, and gently wiped the goo on his own jeans (from Peacocks). This little moment of existence had absolutely no bearing on the rest of universal history. So forget about it, it is literally not going to be a part of this story. It is for this reason that I have never, and *will* never, watch the film *The Butterfly Effect*.

Stardew took the key from Mrs Bambright, inserted it into the ignition, and turned it. A mighty roar sounded and the ship began to vibrate violently. Purple smoke flew out the exhaust, knocking over a group of passing stapenguer school children, sparking many potentially dangerous cell mutations. Stapenguers are very small creatures, about the size of your average insect, and therefore they don't really matter and no one cares if they die. Unless you check your car exhaust for spiders every time you start your car, then you have no right to think that is sad. I bet you don't.

The ship started to lift into the air, and rotated on both its X and Y axes at the same time, in a really cool space-movement. It pointed up into the sky and shot off with a blast. Usually you would fly up a bit higher before doing this bit, but, given the circumstances, Stardew pressed her foot down early. In turn she hit many more stapenguers with the purple smoke and also a load of slightly larger creatures, ones which were about 5 centimetres long, the length a creature has to be before people start to care about its welfare. Stardew didn't care, which was fair enough because there were only 40 seconds until the planet went boom.

BOOM went the entire planet, just 42 seconds later. It was a truly spectacular explosion. Red-hot molten rock flew out at every angle. Creatures burnt up instantly. Cars exploded, wine glasses smashed and babies cried, then died. It was a mess. A few other ships had managed to escape on time, but the death toll was over 400 billion lives (in space, anything living that has a National Insurance number or isn't a plant – Venus fly traps have figured out the National Insurance number application process – counts as a life, so yes, you guessed it, even wasps and stapenguers counted!).

In the way of many explosions, our heroes flew away from the cataclysm at precisely the right moment, however, unlike many other dramatic explosions, our heroes all turned to look directly at it, due to the fact that it looked awesome. What wasn't awesome however is the retinopathy that they suffered as a result, but in the heat of the moment they had no care for permanent retinal damage and simply thought to themselves *that looks awesome.*

If you have ever found yourself sitting in a 2003 – 2012 Fiat Panda (second generation) with too many people, or in a Phonax-5000 spaceship with too many aliens, you will understand just how cramped our heroes were. Bodies everywhere. Limbs, tentacles and fronds flailing all over the place, so you have know idea who, or what, you are touching. Some individuals would find this a titillating circumstance. Of course, we tend not to speak to those kinds of people anymore, do we?

*** 

Twenty minutes or so passed. The ship was pretty speedy and had moved away from the remains of the planet, which was now floating about in a big space-mess that the galactic council would very shortly get complaints about. The group could see stars all around them, and the occasional dwarf planet or asteroid, however for each individual most of their vision was filled up by the body of the alien next to them. It was Biffin Bambright who decided to bring up the most pressing issue, which you may be surprised to hear wasn't the lack of space.

'So, you two, I guess we had better introduce ourselves. My name is Mrs Bambright and this here is my very new acquaintance Martin S. Ronson. What you saw us looking at on the screen of the TrumpDrive™ drive back on Diligord-4 was the contents of a floppy disk that Martin S. Ronson acquired before he landed on our planet.'

Stardew and Martin S. Ronson had noticed each other, and there was definite recognition between the two due to Stardew's very rude interaction earlier on her way from the yoffa shop. Neither of them mentioned anything though and it was never spoken of again.

'Well, I think we can all agree without specific explanation,' Stardew said, 'that what is on that disk is of extreme importance!' She stretched her stretchy neck up slightly, meaning she could get a bit more speech done. It was bloody cramped in this ship.

Biffin continued, trying to stretch one of his many limbs out ever so slightly to avoid the overwhelming onset of cramp.

'Well, it seems apparent to me that the whole fate of the universe depends upon every sentient species gaining knowledge of the contents of this disk.'

'Hmm, you're right,' Stardew said, 'not quite sure how to achieve that though. Maybe we should sit down and have a brainstorm about it all. Unfortunately, I don't have a flip chart in here!'

It was Mr Carmichael's turn to speak. He was looking pretty peeved at the cramped conditions – he was used to a roomy office, or the back or an executive space-taxi.

'Look folks, if we're going to be a universe exploring, floppy-disk toting space-team, we're going to need a bigger ship. It's as simple as that. One where we can sit around playing space-chess and practise our sword fighting.'

'What are you on about Mr Carmichael? What's space-chess? And we don't have any swords!' retorted Stardew.

'Well it's like normal chess, but...'

'Oh whatever, you're right though, we can't travel through space for long periods of time in this ship, my corpreal-tracts are going very numb already.' Mrs Bambright blushed and averted his eyes. Stardew continued. 'The question is, how in space-hell are we going to get a bigger ship?! I left all of my money down on Diligord-4, which is now a pile of rubble.' This was, of course, incorrect, as you can't have piles of anything in space. You can get unfortunately get piles, medically.

'Yes, and I've only come out with a purse full of pocket fluff which I had hoped to use to buy some snacks,' said Mrs Bambright.

'Piracy,' came a small voice from the back of the tiny ship. 'We steal a ship, like pirates.'

Martin S. Ronson hadn't said a word since he had said 'What fortune!' earlier on. Since entering the cramped ship he had been longing for the empty escape pod he'd spent hours and hours on in Chapter Three, but at the same time he was happy to be with his new found friends and finally off on an adventure. He was beginning to realise that finding the floppy disk had changed his whole life. What he didn't know was that finding that floppy disk was also going to change the lives of everyone else in the Universe.

'I like the way you move, little disgusting orb,' shouted Stardew from the driver's seat, 'and I would love to see you dressed up as a little pirate!' Mrs Bambright was slightly jealous at the attention Martin S. Ronson was receiving, but also wouldn't have minded popping a little pirate's hat and cutlass on the orb.

Martin S. Ronson did not find this funny.

'Look, I'm serious! We fly towards the next comfy, spacious ship we see, approach it like friendly aliens, and once we are on board, BAM! We take the ship and fling the previous owners out into space. Badda-bing, badda-boom. Then we kick back with a G&T and play space-*Snakes and Ladders* like Mr Carmichael said.'

'CHESS!' Mr Carmichael shot back. 'Snakes and Ladders is an abhorrent game, which requires no skill whatsoever and simply relies on the roll of a dice. You might as well sell your copy of the game and flip a coin to see who would have won.'

Everybody went quiet for a little bit.

'Anyway, let's find us a ship!' exclaimed Mrs Bambright.

*The escape from Diligord-4 prior to its destruction*

# Six

It was a beautiful morning in space. The local sun was burning on the surface at 9,400 degrees celsius and there wasn't a cloud in the sky, because it was space. At a distance of 1.4 billion kilometres from the sun, a Mark 2 Excus Philanthropist Adventure Cruiser was cruising on by (think suburban Land Rover Defender, clean as a whistle, but with the potential to do so much more than pick Bianca and Rupert up from school when there's a perfectly adequate (and electric powered) school bus put on by the council).

'Totty! Totty, fetch me another hot towel dear,' asked a large, flabby alien male. He hadn't always been this flabby, but he'd let himself go in recent years. In his early twenties he was a real buff ting, all hair gel and muscle, and he had his pick of the ladies. He chose Totty, and she had felt like the luckiest girl in the world.

Now it was a different story. He'd got a few promotions at work and his stress levels had gone through the roof. He stopped working out and he started drinking too much. Before long his muscles were a distant memory, replaced with swathes of rippling fat. When he walked, his folds danced like a sky full of starlings, intertwined, evolving, beautiful.

Totty had had enough of her slob of a man. He was rarely at home, and when he was at home his mind was still in the office. And she knows what he's been doing with Charlene, the pretty back-end developer on the fifth floor. Disgusting things. She'd been reading his text messages. She'd given up so much for him, and this is how he repaid her?! The camel's back had been broken by the weight of this last straw, to use the cliché.

'Hot towel, Totty! Please! And a straw, I think there's one left, in that camel shaped jar!' The flabby alien lent over, picked up the remote and switched on his favourite Alanis Morissette album.

She shuddered. Today was the day she planned to kill her husband. She was going to take the wheel of the Mark 2 Excus Philaonthropist Adventure Cruiser and slam the thing into an oncoming space-lorry. She knew she'd probably die too, but she'd bought really good health insurance that puts your consciousness into the body of a well loved pet, which was an upgrade on her life right now.

Her hand slowly moved towards the steering wheel.

Suddenly, an almighty crash erupted from the back of the vehicle.

It was their adopted pheeleotarp son, Gregory. He had dropped a pile of plates.

'Goddamnit, Gregory!' screamed Totty. She'd forgotten that he was in the car as well, which is terrible parenting, especially when you're about to make movements to destroy that car and everybody within it. She couldn't kill

Gregory, despite his lack of respect for crockery. Usually Gregory would respond to admonishment from his mother, but his face was firmly focused on something else.

There was a small, floating, orangey-purple orb hovering just in front of his nose. Now, Gregory had seen his fair share of floating orbs in his time, I mean, show us a teenager who hasn't, but this one was different. This one was wearing a tiny pirate outfit.

'Erm, Mum... Dad...' he started, 'there's a small floating orb dressed as a pirate back here...'

'Huh. That's ironic,' replied his flabby father, who paused his favourite album to attend to the commotion.

The small floating orb, as you may have guessed, was none other than Martin S. Ronson. If you *hadn't* guessed that, then I recommend you put this book/audiobook/movie down and go and read something else, you're obviously not following. Now, Martin S. Ronson was too small to be an intimidating force, but what he lacked in size, he made up for in ingenuity.

'Hello, small pirate,' said the flabby father. 'How are you today?'

'Silence!' screamed Martin S. Ronson. He had vowed to never kill a man, but had no issues with threats to kill a man. 'Silence, or you die!'

'I think you should keep talking, honey,' quipped Totty.

'And you, formerly attractive woman! This is a lovely, practical, family space vehicle, and I'm afraid I must take it for my own. It's even covered in the finest shards of crockery, exactly how I like my transport. Please exit the vehicle immediately, and nobody shall be harmed.'

The flabby father was not amused.

'I'm sorry small pirate, but this is *my* practical family space vehicle, and you're really not very threatening.' He retook his seat. 'In fact, I'm finding this whole situation incredibly amusing.'

Rats. Martin S. Ronson had to get scarier. But how?

'As you wish, flabby man. As you wish.'

He was stalling for time. His new comrades would be at the back of the vehicle imminently, and they were a lot scarier than he was.

'As… you… wish.'

They family stared blankly at the golplorx. Gregory went to clean up the plates.

'As… you…'

Another almighty crash interrupted Martin S. Ronson's elongated sentence. The back of the cruiser was completely destroyed.

'Stardew!' screamed Mr Carmichael. 'You weren't supposed to crash into the vehicle! Now it's of no use to us!'

'I didn't mean to! They must have backed into us!' replied

Stardew, daughter of the king (in case you'd forgotten).

'They did not! You really are a terrible driver!'

Martin S. Ronson finished his sentence.

'...wish.'

The flabby man's eyes had opened wide with terror.

'Do you have any money?' the orb asked.

'I do,' replied the flabby man.

'Well, drive us to the Intergalactic Car Exchange. It looks like you're going to have to buy us both reasonably priced used vehicles.'

The flabby man nodded. He didn't want to mess with *this* group of rogue space pirates. They appeared to both mean business, and have a terrible lack of driving ability. He then decided to take out a life insurance policy on the group and buy them a reasonably priced used vehicle, as anybody who drove with such a lack of ability surely couldn't last particularly long on the highways of space.

The (actual) irony was not lost on Martin S. Ronson. He'd left the golplorx life of ship invasion behind to be a better citizen of the universe, but now here he was, sitting in the back of a car that he had forcibly seized. This made him feel quite sad. But, however, he did have in his possession a very important floppy disk, which meant he had to bend the rules. He decided that if he continued to only bend the rules, rather than break them completely, he would be able to live with himself after this whole sorry affair. I don't know if you've ever tried to bend the rules, but they are actually rather elastic.

I also don't know if you've ever been to an Intergalactic Car Exchange, but they are fascinating places. Vehicles from all over the place arrive there. Some big, some small, some just right.

Martin S. Ronson jabbed the flabby man in the back, forcing him forward to a car that Martin S. Ronson considered 'just right'. In its interior it had a lovely lounge area, with an open plan kitchen and a ping pong table. Down the hall was a Zen garden. Perfection.

'How much?' he asked.

'25,000' replied a rather attractive glorp from behind a counter. The glorp had juice dribbling down his front. Just like in the magazines.

'Very reasonable,' replied Martin S. Ronson. 'Can you stretch to that flabby man?'

'I guess so. And by the way, I do have a name! It's Mr Flarbimarn.'

'Okay Flarbimarn, pop in your intergalactic credit card and buy it!'

He bought it. Intergalactic credit cards work everywhere in the entire universe apart from Germany, who have been slow to retrofit existing payment machines.

Meanwhile, Mr Carmichael had been speaking to Totty and they were getting on well. She had been explaining the woes of being married to a flabby man and having an adopted son who drops plates. Mr Carmichael was a very caring man as you can tell, and offered all kinds of advice, but in the end it wasn't really his place to interfere in other people's relationships. Mr Carmichael let the couple go off together after the piracy was done and they had a lovely new, second hand, space car.

Ultimately, this resulted in Flarbimarn the flabby man's death, as Totty melted him down to use as biofuel about 1.5 million miles from the Intergalactic Car Exchange. This was a truly horrendous thing to happen and *even* Floobidan Flarbimarn the flabby man didn't deserve it.

In their haste to get away, the couple had left their adopted son Gregory in the toilets, which at first seemed a very sad thing for him, but he ended up selling cars for another 20 years before dying of natural causes on the 22nd of November. He enjoyed his life and eventually, after 7 weeks, had forgotten his adoptive parents' faces. At one time he thought he might try and seek them out across the galaxy and have his own space adventure, but he had too much of his adoptive father's blood in him and ended up sitting around enjoying a hot towel. He never dropped another plate in his life.

Our group of heroes readied themselves, buying crisps, chocolate and lucozade, and took their seats in their new ship. It was actually Stardew who suggested that Mr Carmichael drive away and set them up for autopilot. Maybe she was realising that she wasn't a fantastic driver after all.

*The careless destruction of plates by Gregory*

5 + 3 − 1

You may think that space food has to be different from planet food. Wrong. It's all a lie. In an attempt to slow the increase in astronaut applications, the Earth organisation NASA told everyone that space food had to be small and dry and shit. Ice cream which was just dried blocks, rehydratable Ramen noodles, and dried saag aloo. In actual fact, you can eat anything you like in space. This statement was happily proven by our gang of adventurers in their ship when they sat down to a traditional roast blarksnan with all the trimmings (after the chocs, crisps and lucozade had run out from when they swung by a hypermarket in the Ecalpmodnar Cluster).

After the meal was done and everybody had a content belly, Stardew stood up from her comfy space sofa.

'Right then, I'm the daughter of the king, and I thereby make myself leader of this group. We have a very important job ahead of us and it all revolves around that floppy disk that little Martin S. Ronson has got with him.'

'I'd prefer you not to refer to me as 'little' Stardew, I find it patronising and condescending,' the cute little orb replied.

'Very well. First thing's first though, we need to decide where we are going.'

Mrs Bambright interjected.

'Sorry for interjecting Miss Stardew, but I have an

obligation to fulfill. When I met Martin S. Ronson he was asking me to carry out the duty of my employment and sort him out with a body, and I intend to do just that.'

'Very well,' replied Stardew, 'but how are we going to do that when your workshop has been blown to smithereens?'

'Well, I don't know much about smithereening, but I do know bodies, and I'm fairly certain that I can whip something up using one of the ship's spacesuits, a tool box and some alien knowhow!'

Martin S. Ronson and Mrs Bambright left the table and proceeded to a back room where some spacesuits were kept. These were cool spacesuits. Like in many new sci-fi films, they were similar to the kind of space suit used on Earth, but they were shinier in places, more slick, had better colours, and had a lovely big round face part that shone a light directly into the wearers eyes, which would be useless in space but lets the cinemagoer see the wearer's beautiful cheekbones.

'How would you like to be in one of those, Martin S. Ronson?'

'I think that would be totally out of this world!' replied the small orb.

Mrs Bambright pulled some tools out from the toolbox. A long screwdriver, some tape, a Trevor key (an Allen key with six sides) and a nice healthy looking bunch of silicon chips and circuit boards. He got to work.

Martin S. Ronson watched patiently, amazed at the knowledge that Mrs Bambright had in his leathery head, and the skill he could muster through his large oily hands. The spacesuit had been opened out and Biffin Bambright was building and installing complicated looking artificial nerves and mechanical functions, all of which would be controlled by Martin S. Ronson's small but nimble mind upon completion.

Every eight or nine minutes, Mrs Bambright would require Martin S. Ronson to climb into the helmet of the suit, fasten himself in, and have a go at functioning the arms and legs using his mind. There were a few malfunctions along the way, including one instance where Martin S. Ronson undecidedly stuck his new middle finger up at Mrs Bambright. Awkward! They knew they were making good progress when he was able to make the suit perform the first three moves in the Macarena. At this point they decided to take a break.

'Mrs Bambright, I've got something I think I need to get off my chest, and now seems like a good time.'

Mrs Bambright sighed. He had seen this coming for a while now and hadn't been looking forward to it. The golplorx continued.

'I'm not sure I trust Stardew with what I saw on that

floppy disk, and I'm concerned about the direction our adventure might take if we all pursue this together.'

It had not been the thing Biffin Bambright had been expecting, and he was surprised to find himself a little sad that it hadn't been.

'Hmm,' he replied. 'I know what you mean little buddy, but I think we've been given an opportunity here to change the course of the galaxy. If we don't at least try, how are we to live with ourselves if the worst does come to pass? I was very happy with my life in my Bodyshop back on Diligord-4, but now that it's no longer in existence, I feel a freedom in the way my course has shifted. I now have the opportunity to live my life as each day comes and see the galaxy for what it really is. Also, I had three overdue library books that I had misplaced, my laptop couldn't run the latest update because I didn't have enough memory left to install it, and I was bored of feeding and cleaning my pet fish for very little reward. So in a way, I say we have to just roll with it and see what happens. I guess you could say I'm a bit of an ubifloon.'

'An ubifloon, what's that?' replied Martin S. Ronson, quizzically.

'Oh sorry, Diligord-4 vernacular and all that. Well, back on Diligord-4 we tend to call people –'

'What are you on about, *tentacle people*?! You don't

have tentacles…'

'No, I said *tend to call* people… look, this is getting confusing, let me tell you a little story.'

'Okay,' replied Martin S. Ronson.

'I didn't always live on Diligord-4. In fact, back in my younger days I was a planet hopper. I only stayed on a planet for about six months at a time. I was younger and hip, I had hair back then, and believed in the freedom of life and taking the time to enjoy everything that the universe has to offer.'

Martin S. Ronson was going to interject and make a comment about how the universe is so ridiculously big that there's no point in trying to enjoy everything it has to offer as you will always fall short of that goal. He didn't say anything though.

'One time I found myself on the planet Shralwrinkal which, you may know, has a reputation as a bit of a party planet. I had been living there for about three months, partying every single night and sleeping in the day, occasionally going hunting in the vast jungle land that surrounded the planet's capital city, Doostjals.

This one time I was out hunting with my best friend Horatio, you know, fully camouflaged and wearing nothing but our windhags to keep us warm. We had spotted a plump histobear down by the river a few days earlier and had been tracking it day and night, sleeping in turns. This bear had plump fronds and looked delicious. We were desperate to be seen by the ladies hauling it back to town for a feast, and to then carry on partying.

It was on the fourth day that Horatio thought he had an opening to trap the histobear. He got up and set a snare right by the opening to the cave where this bear had been sleeping. It was a foolproof plan – the bear must leave the cave from the front, and when it did... BAM, we would have it. Then straight back to party town to get on those beers and shots. Am I right?'

'Yes,' was all Martin S. Ronson could say.

'So, the next morning we both got up and moved towards the cave. We could see the histobear right where we wanted it, in the trap! Horatio was all like '*I told you so*' and to be fair to him, he had told me. So, as we approached the bear, carefully, one step at a time, we were suddenly whipped up in a frenzy and found ourselves dangling in a net, right above the bear, right next to our very own trap. After a moment of shock we looked at the bear, who met our gaze. A rustle came from the cave and out came two younger histobears, chuckling to themselves. It was at this moment that realisation came to us. The hunters had become the hunted! Panic overcame Horatio and he started screaming. Regardless of this, I still took the opportunity to say to him *'you told me what?'*

Biffin Bambright paused and looked up towards the ceiling, breathing inward. He was collecting his thoughts *and* his composure.

'In the net that encased us both, I managed to reach behind my youthful and muscular body and grabbed my knife. After a few moments I cut us free. The two of us fell to the floor, right on our bums. We regained our footing as the two histobears charged towards us. I took my chance and pushed Horatio right into their path. I then turned and ran as fast as I could, making it back to the bar with ten minutes of happy hour left. Horatio was never seen again.'

A single tear ran down Biffin's face, and then another. He was crying.

Martin S. Ronson had no idea what to think. This was nuts. He couldn't believe the amazing character backstory he had just heard. It gave Mrs Bambright depth and interest. He reached out and gently patted his pal on the shoulder. Not really knowing the point that the story was making, still not knowing what an ubifloon was, and correctly hoping that it would never enter into this story again, he figured out something to say.

'Okay Mrs Bambright, I guess you're right. I spent so long floating around the air ducts of Captain Morf's ship that I think I'd forgotten to trust people and leave things to fate.' However, deep in his heart he still had a little doubt. And a little doubt can go a long way.

Mrs Bambright and Martin S. Ronson returned to the ship's bridge to speak to the rest of their team. They walked into the room just as Mr Carmichael was finishing a witty anecdote with an ambiguous ending that made everyone laugh.

'So I said the to the desk clerk, *'never ask a phalzarian for a new tie, unless you want to be picking up the pieces!'*'

Stardew burst into laughter. She turned around and ceased her laugh instantly. She stared at Martin S. Ronson in his newly acquired body, his small real body floating in the helmet.

'Wow! You look great! How does it feel to have a fully functioning body?'

'Well,' said Martin S. Ronson, 'I must say, it feels fantastic!'

Mrs Bambright obviously had something on his mind.

'Look, it's about time we decided exactly where we are heading, and why!'

'We know *exactly* where we are headed, Mrs Bambright. It turns out that I have a secret, long lost, twin brother.'

'What's that got to do with anything, Mr Carmichael?'

'Well, back in the '80s he was a right whizz in pirate movie sharing, and although floppy disks were far too small to hold a movie, he did dabble in the piracy of sharing documents no larger than 1.44 megabytes. We are going to track him down and make loads of copies of this floppy disk to disperse around the galaxy, and save the planet!'

'Which planet?' replied Mrs Bambright.

'I don't know, it's just a figure of speech!'

'Gotcha!' shouted Mrs Bambright, who then hit the big green GO button on the dashboard. Nothing happened because the coordinates hadn't been set yet. Mr Carmichael shuffled over.

'Allow me.'

He punched in some obscure coordinates, getting the next stage of their adventure off to a tremendous start.

However, our fabled hero (and personally our favourite character) Martin S. Ronson was feeling a little down. He had seen what was on the that floppy disk, and he knew how important it was to forcibly share it with the entire universe, but he wasn't sure why they were in such a hurry. The problem he was finding was that they weren't aware of any imminent danger. The destruction of the universe didn't seem apparent or threatening enough. This made him uneasy. Our heroes had no nemesis to fear and battle. Martin S. Ronson was thinking, who, what, where, when and why was their antagonist? And how?

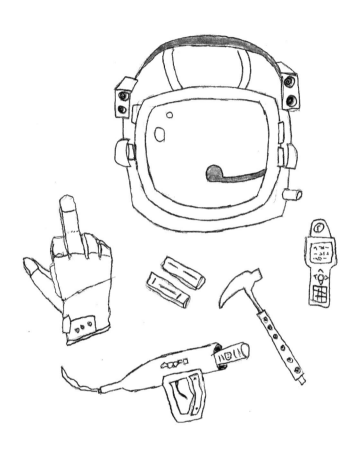

*Bashin' out a body with Biffin Bambright*

# Space-Interlude

*The following story takes place centuries before our intrepid travellers walked their respective planets. Many stories of this era were lost to the ages. We only know of these tales because they were captured in great detail on a state-of-the-art, high definition CCTV system, which was stored on a 120 TB hard drive and backed up daily in* The Cloud.

***

It was black. It was black, and dark and grim. It was black, and dark and grim and Gorgol was trudging down a long, helical staircase (which is different to a spiral staircase, as you well know). He was trudging slowly, using an old wooden cane to steady himself on each step. It was no way to live, not in this day and age.

That is because there was no day, and no age at all. The place we have found ourselves in was one of the most desolate and unwelcoming places in the universe. And it's not even in *this* universe! In this vile and despicable place, there are no comforts at all. No tea, and certainly no biscuits. Everything was kind of wobbly, and everything was black, and dark, and grim.

In all the history of time – which you have no real idea about because all your clocks are wrong and your calendars are rubbish – this really grim place has only connected to our third dimension twice. Once was when the floppy disk that has become so integral to this story was leaked out of a dimensional crack (which may be the subject of a prequel novel should this one go extremely well). The other time is explained in the part of this book that you are reading right now.

Gorgol sniffed and huffed as he finally made it to the bottom of the helical stairs.

'What a bloody nightmare,' he moaned, which was a strange thing to say, as this place was a bloody nightmare all of the time, so it was quite normal.

His master was in the next room. Gorgol breathed in deeply and pushed the heavy door open. He was hit by an unbearable and vomit inducing stench that filled the room. And this was really saying something, as the whole of this reality was pretty stinky. Wiping vomit from his chin, the gargoyley demon stepped into the throne room.

The throne room was incredibly large – a cube which measured 60 metres in each dimension, including time. Along the floor, walls and ceiling was beautiful, hand-crafted oak panelling, gilded in each corner. Piles and piles of treasure were scattered around the room in a wanton fashion, each pile containing a small, gold dwelling alien called a forex, which swam around, slowly ingesting the mound of loot that housed it. This didn't worry anybody whose treasure had been infected, as a plump forex was worth much more than a measly pile of treasure, and tasted just as good.

The throne was in the dead centre of the cube, levitating so its midpoint was 30 metres in the air. Gorgol's master was sitting in the throne, eyes closed, humming the tune to *Stay Another Day* by East 17. The stench was, in fact, coming from this levitating tycoon, rather than the room itself. For the last one hundred years, the Master had chosen to wash in gold rather than with soap and water, and that doesn't really work. At all.

A dozen forex were scuttling around Gorgol's feet, hoping that he was carrying a trove of gold, or at least gold leaf, that he might accidentally drop to the floor for them to feast on. It was not gold, however, that he was carrying. No.

Gorgol continued walking until he stood directly underneath his master's levitating chair. There was only one way to get the Master to come back down to ground level, and that was to sing the special song:

'*Master, Master,*
*Up so far in the sky.*
*Master, Master,*
*How did you get so high?*

*Master, tell me,*
*How does your chair levitate?*
*Master, oh Master,*
*I really think you should come down.'*

The Master then screams the following:

*'I SHALL NEVER TELL YOU MY SECRETS,*
*YOU DAMNED DECREPID FOOL,*
*WHERE IS MY SOUP?'*

And with that, the ritual is done. The Master is then immediately at ground level. There's no transition, the chair is just immediately on the ground, in a really spooky, horror film, jump cut fashion. That's why Gorgol had to dance to the side of the room during his song, lest he be crushed.

'Is that my soup, Gorgol?' the Master asked.

'It is.'

It was a space-leek and potato soup, which Gorgol had cooked himself.

'It smells very tasty,' said the Master.

'I hope you enjoy it.'

The Master did not enjoy it. Gorgol turned from his master and began walking back to the door, to start the extremely long journey back up the hideous staircase to the kitchen where he made the soup. The journey up the stairs would be long, treacherous and incredibly, incredibly dull. It would take so long that stars would be born and die during the time it took to complete the journey, and whole civilisations would be created, evolve, eventually invent small collectable figurines for children, and then burn in a haze of apocalyptic thunder. Flipping ages.

The worst thing about this was that when he eventually got back to the kitchen, it would be about dinner time, and he'd need to bring back more soup. There were many reasons why the kitchen was so far away that are not necessary to explain here. Again, they may form some part of the prequel novel/fan fiction/erotica.

As Gorgol reached the door, the Master took the spoon and dipped it into the soup. The spoon, now full of delicious soup, was stirred three times, tapped against the side of the bowl, and then lifted to the Master's mouth. At this moment, a huge blast of pure, white, unadulterated light shot out from the soup bowl. It flew directly into Gorgol's hairy, spotty and sweaty back, giving him a nasty rash. The spoon shot forwards at the speed of space and Gorgol unwittingly caught it with his right hand (he was left handed).

'Oh my!' cried Gorgol, as he was lifted into the air by the beam of light, which had now become adulterated.

'M-m-m-master! What is happening?' he called out. The

Master said nothing, simply holding the soup bowl steady.

Gorgol managed to turn around by flailing his arms wildly, like you do when you're standing on a spinny chair at work, reaching for something on a top shelf and trying to use all your knowledge of physics and spinning to grab it. If you knew more physics, you'd refer to it as *angular momentum*, but you don't, which is why you usually fall off your chair at this point. As the beam held him steady in the air, all kinds of goo and gunge started to fly off the beam (this was the adulterated part). As the goo and gunge hit the ground, it started to burn through the hardwood flooring, hissing as it went. The whole room was vibrating and the forex were going nutso. Gold pieces were dropping from the ceiling and the forex were lapping it up, but they were also really scared, so were scurrying about.

This was not good. Gorgol glanced up at his master who he had served for all eternity. The Master met his glance with a slight smirk and then a wink. With that wink, Gorgol disappeared.

Gorgol had left not only the throne room, but the dimension. Little did he know (how would he have known?), his existence would one day become intertwined with a certain little charismatic floating orb, named Martin S. Ronson.

The Master reopened one winking eye. The main

reason the Master hadn't got to enjoy the soup was because when Gorgol was transported, the soup bowl exploded, and the soup went all over the Master's face, shirt and, *embarrassingly*, trousers. This would eventually add to the horrendous stench, because washing yourself in gold does nothing to clean off soup.

The Master, infuriated, was aware of how long it takes to get food delivered, so made a quick call to the kitchen and ordered more leek and space-potato soup. Unfortunately, another spoon was not added to the order, which eventually caused no end of despair.

After this, the Master sat up, and rubbing two hands together, spoke quietly to the room in a menacing voice.

'So, the time has come. The Spoon of Valaxion has risen, and has chosen none other than Gorgol to unite the spheres, find the crystal, and bring destruction to all who stand in our way!'

*The most important soup you'll ever see*

# Chapter 第八章

In a rather muscular and tattooed spiral arm of the galaxy (it's worth noting that the tattoos were quite trendy and 'with the time', not old with faded colours or anything), in a solar system with a surprising number of nudist planets, there was a comedy club called *The Chuckling Paediatrician*. You could find this comedy club on an asteroid that was making its way around the solar system in a large orbit. Tickets are a nightmare to get hold of at certain times during its orbital cycle, however they reserve a number for students and customers with at least four flailing-goondges for a special price. At other times, it's very easy to get a ticket. The club is closed on Mondays. They do not have a fax machine.

On this particular day there was a very old and sad looking comedian on stage, performing to a hen party who were somewhat disappointed with the chief bridesmaid for picking this as their activity. Everyone knows that during years 60-78 of the asteroid's orbital cycle the line-up was always crap, because at this time the asteroid was in close proximity to the planet Selppinegral, which had an horrendous odour, so horrendous that it was able to travel through space all the way to *The Chuckling Paediatrician*. This explains why everyone at the club with a nose also had a peg placed upon it, free of charge, in a bid to gain more customers.

The old and sad looking comedian was doing his best

to tell some jokes and make the ladies laugh. It wasn't really working. The hen party was a beautiful mix of space-races. There were five of them. The bride-to-be, Claire, was a nexum who worked in a bank that only sold loans to people who resembled celebrities. The chief bridesmaid was a rather buxom jotaj, whose suckers were something to behold. Her name was Phyllis. The three other bridesmaids were a pancake-shaped pooldan with stubby legs named Reesen, a criterion named Shona, and an alsatian named Bruce. Shona looked very much like Felicity Jones and had met Claire at the bank. Bruce had also met Claire at the bank when she was denied a loan while dressed as Hugh Fearnley-Whittingstall. The two had of course hit it off immediately.

Claire was getting married the next morning in a beautiful town hall in Space-Islington. Everything was paid for, the flowers, the jazz band, the jazz-fusion band, the indian-fusion wedding breakfast, the priest, the priest's hand, the vicar, the vicarage insurance, the beads, oh my god so many beads, H from Steps was going to be there, two elephants were going to fight to the death, Dwayne 'The Rock' Johnson was doing a speech and then there were the centrepieces.

It was an expensive wedding, but Claire's new husband was none other than space-famous Troy McClusky, the universe's second most successful entrepreneur. The most successful was Danny Dyer, who had discovered a new way of making paint that was much better than the old way. NO, not your Danny Dyer, SPACE-Danny Dyer! Your Danny Dyer is from London, not space.

The sad old comedian was telling another joke.

'Three bloosnacks walk into a bar!'

Everyone laughed. This was the first funny thing he'd said all night.

Almost at once, the wall furthest from the stage collapsed in a massive collapsing. Behind it was a big, fat, dirty, cylindrical head.

'SHIT!' exclaimed the head. 'I am never letting Mr Carmichael drive again!'

Nobody knows why Mr Carmichael drove so badly, he used to be an excellent driver. In fact, he used to be called Mr Michael until everyone saw how good at driving he was, then they called him Mr 'Car' Michael and that evolved into his current name, Mr 'Car' Carmichael. Oh how the mighty do fall.

Fortunately, nobody was hurt. Unfortunately, Mr Carmichael was left handed and tried to reverse, but accidentally jolted forwards with the accelerator. They jolted directly into Claire, Troy McClusky's impending wife, and provided such equal horizontal and vertical forces (which added up to 45 degrees) that she was launched directly into the air and off the asteroid, ages away from *The Chuckling Paediatrician*. As she floated off into space, her blood began to boil and evaporate. The air from her lungs expanded and was pulled into the vacuum, causing her lungs to rupture. She then began to freeze solid. She was dead. Actually dead, she's not coming back into this story. Her body floated around in space for flipping ages. Mr Carmichael is now probably guilty of manslaughter. Anyway.

Bruce howled tears of sadness at the loss of her best friend. Reesen dropped to her knees, her fluffy pink tiara falling to the floor, and she cried in anguish. Phyllis looked around in shock and tried to squeeze out a tear. Shona downed her WKD and pegged it out of the club, never to be seen again. Nobody else cared, and the comedian told another terrible joke. Martin S. Ronson did care a bit, but he didn't want to be seen as a wuss. There is a major, toxic masculinity problem in and around space.

Importantly though, the ship our heroes were travelling on was now royally fucked. It was a complete write off. Nobody was driving off in that, even if they were 60 times better at driving than Mr Carmichael. Mr Flarbimarn the flabby man who'd bought them the car had got space insurance to cover such events, however none of the group had the policy number or knew who to call.

The police swiftly arrived. Despite the obvious signs signalling Claire's death, they were there to enforce the incredibly strict parking laws on the asteroid. These were the parking police and they only cared about parking. If you've ever tried to pick someone up at Heathrow Airport and gone to the 'drop off' zone, you know EXACTLY what I mean. The other police departments had no budgets after the cuts that had happened the previous year. Due to this, everybody got away with everything on the asteroid. Everything *except* bad parking!

Suddenly, the front door to the club opened and the daughter of the king strolled in, followed by an elderly man in handcuffs, himself followed by four police officers of varying degrees of alien, all with pegs upon their varying alien noses. The gaggle of bridesmaids were still on the floor crying and breathing heavily as they came to terms with the short and horrendous death of their friend Claire. Troy had been space-telephoned and was on his way. He was secretly glad Claire had been killed in an accident, as he didn't really want to marry her. He had mistaken her for someone else seven years ago but was too embarrassed to own up to it. He was now free to watch *our* Danny Dyer's back-catalogue on Netflix in his underpants again on Saturdays.

The daughter of the king and her cuffed companion,

Carmichael, carefully criss-crossed the comedy club, chased courageously by the cops. Bruce bashfully barked and bit the bastards badly, bruising their bottoms. The daughter of the king, who was one tough cookie, kicked the alsation square in the face. The dog then flew through the air and landed at the feet of the parking police. This also counted as a parking violation, as Bruce was in fancy dress as a pick-up truck for the redneck-themed hen party.

The parking police lifted their batons and surrounded the daughter of the king and Mr Carmichael. They all rushed towards them in a well rehearsed manoeuvre, ready to bash some bloody heads in for not respecting the green cross code. Stardew had other plans, and with one carefully weighted 360 degree roundhouse kick, disposed of the whole unit. Now not even parking could be enforced on this god forsaken asteroid. The police officers were all on the floor clutching their wounds, just like in the Batman video game where one or two punches gets rid of an enemy forever. One of them, Seth, radioed over to his good friend in the 'team-who-rescue-police-who've-been-injured' team. However, due to the aforementioned budget cuts, they didn't have their radios charged and therefore did not come. This was a weekly occurrence. Austerity doesn't work.

The bouquet of bridesmaids/gaggle of hens looked at each other. What the hell was going on here? Five minutes ago they were enjoying themselves on a dull hen night, and now their 'hen' was clucking dead, Bruce was unconscious and the traffic police – the highest order of law in the land – were also conked out.

But enough about them. Our team were here to find Mr Carmichael's long lost twin brother. Fortunately, literally everybody on the asteroid was in the comedy club, as this was the only mildly good thing there was to do. Mr Carmichael began to scan the crowd. The comedian told another joke.

'So, the thing about Blergmeignians is... right... and I'm not a racist but I tell it how it is... right... they're all on benefits aren't they? Never worked a day in their life a Blergmeignian. No madam it's true, it's true. I know some lovely Blergmeignians myself too but you know, you go into their shops and you feel like you are no longer in your beautiful homeland where everything is right and proper but in some foreign place where the food gives you a stomach ache. I do like a nice, mild Blergmeignian stew on occasion, but you know, we have their recipes now, they can go home!'

Our heroes looked at each other. This was obviously Mr Carmichael's long lost, racist, twin brother. It was amazing how two brothers brought up in the same household could have such differing opinions about Blergmeignia. Also, it was easy to tell they were twins as they were dressed identically.

Corey Carmichael was so engrossed in his own joke and was so sad and old that he hadn't even realised the mayhem that had been taking place around him. He looked up, hoping to see how his joke was going down. He looked at the school of bridesmaids, noticing that the buxom one was missing. He saw Martin S. Ronson in his shiny new body and Mrs Bambright with his lovely shaped head. He then saw the one person he vowed he would never see again, Mr Carmichael.

Instantly, Corey dropped his mic in the shittest mic-drop you've ever seen (it bounced off his knee), and he slithered to the back door of the club.

Our heroes gave chase to the racist sibling and arrived at the door within seconds. They flung the lovely, oak door outwards into the glistening car park and hurriedly ran across the threshold. What they weren't expecting was that on the other side of the door was a water slide (like you get at center parcs). In single file they were battered and bruised down the blue plastic tube, water filling their ears and nostrils and mouths and anuses, until they were thrown out of the end like a letter in a old movie that depicted letters in the future being transported around in tubes, except it malfunctioned and just lobbed the letter out at the end. Stardew's bikini flew off and Mrs Bambright blushed.

Our heroes ran. Oh, how they ran. Through the park, through the fields, through the shopping mall. Unfortunately for Corey Carmichael, he was old and slow, and Martin S. Ronson was getting more confident with his newly acquired body.

'Go go gadget arms!' he shouted at the top of his voice. Nothing happened, he wasn't that well acquainted. Instead he just pressed the mind-button with his mind and his left arm extended, whipping Corey's right foot out from under him. As Corey span round he caught a glimpse of Martin S. Ronson's golplorxian face through the glass of the spacesuit and gave him a very shocked look. Wouldn't you?

CRASH!

FACEPLANT!

And he was down.

Stardew was the first to reach him. She turned him over to talk to him. Unfortunately, he was the right way up before she turned him, so she had to turn him over again.

'WHERE'S THE BOMB?!' she shouted. He looked at her blankly. Then she remembered what was going on and said, slightly more calmly,

'Corey Carmichael. Your brother has been in the service of my family for over twenty years. It is now your time to come to the aid of your king and make some copies of this floppy disk!'

'What floppy disk?' croaked the more racist of the two Carmichaels.

'Martin S. Ronson! Show him the goods!'

Martin S. Ronson took the floppy disk from his floppy disk holder, which was embedded in his new thigh. He presented it to Corey Carmichael, who gave it a sniff, all the while keeping one suspicious eye on our hero of all heroes, Martin S. Ronson. All his years of floppy disk replication had given him the ability to read data from floppy disks with all six of his senses, including that one where you feel like you're being watched.

His eyes widened. Those ones and zeroes (and the occasional two somehow) smelt strange. The strangest smell the stranger had smelled. His eyes widened again.

'Jesus, guys! This is some pretty heavy stuff you want to disseminate! Are you sure about this?!'

Stardew barked back, defiantly.

'YOU BET YOUR TWIN ASS IT IS!'

Corey jumped up.

'I haven't spoken to my brother in over twenty years. AND I AM *NOT* GOING TO START NOW!'

He dribbled slightly.

'Very well, take us to your home.'

'My home is miles away, do you have a car?'

'Our car is out of action right now. Let's walk!'

'I'm not sure I can, I'm pretty old and sad you see…'

'Fine,' said Stardew, exasperated. 'Let's find ourselves a new vehicle.' She'd also realised that no matter where Corey's house was, you just can't walk about in space.

At this moment, Troy McClusky landed with an almighty crash next to *The Chuckling Pediatrician* in his space-limousine. He landed on a gradient and the car slid comically slowly down the hill and came to a stop next to our band of merry men and women. The back door opened.

'Where is the love of my life who I'm totally in love with, Claire?!'

Mr Carmichael vomited.

'I'm so sorry sir. I accidentally shunted her into space and she is no longer with us. I wish this hadn't happened, but it has. Is there anything I can do to make it up to you?!'

Troy thought about how he was supposed to react in this situation, as what he wanted to do was give Mr Carmichael a great big kiss on the lips.

'I need to fight you! To the death!'

Troy immediately regretted saying this. He was scared, and could feel the fear building up in him. He was more scared than a man having a wee at a slightly blocked urinal which has just started to flush, causing the shallow bowl of the urinal to fill up faster than it should due to the urine and the slight blockage.

As the figurative urine reached breaking point and started to overflow, dripping onto Troy's literal shoes, Stardew took an aggressive stance. She'd already knocked out the whole fleet of traffic police AND three Bacardi and cokes while nobody was looking. What was one entrepreneur?

Troy also took an aggressive stance, but aimed himself towards Mr Carmichael. As he readied his fist and Mr Carmichael braced himself for impact, Stardew wound up her hind leg, and thrust it towards Troy's perfect chin. His head exploded. Luckily for Troy, his second head was fine. That's right, Troy McClusky had two heads, and one of them was detachable! He rolled it out from behind him and threw it at Stardew. It hit her straight in the shoulder and flipped her around. Troy's head bounced back onto his neck.

'That do anything for you?' he said.

'No,' replied Stardew. Meanwhile, Mr Carmichael had legged it to Troy's car and opened his glove compartment.

'Jackpot!' he cried, as he pulled out what he thought could be a winning lottery ticket. 'Jackpot!' he cried once more, pulling out a large space-rifle. He waltzed over to Troy and shot him square in the second head.

'Heads up!' he chuckled.

'Jackpot!' replied Stardew, also chuckling. She noticed

a tiny little piece of Troy McClusky's second skull had embedded itself in the palm of her hand, but it hadn't caused her any pain. She blinked and it had vanished.

'Weird,' she said to herself. This is one of those things that does come back into the story, so you'd better remember it.

Troy's lifeless body had fallen into the pit at the end of the waterslide, and when morning came around would cause a blockage of school-aged children.

\*\*\*

Now, space limousines are nice. Really nice. You may have been in a limousine yourself and thought 'Hey, this is nice!', but that's nothing compared to Troy McClusky's limousine. It had cup holders everywhere, a swimming pool and sauna, a small cinema, two tennis courts, a games room and a vending machine.

Stardew reached into Troy's back pocket and pulled out his keys.

'Now we're cooking,' she said. The crew and Corey Carmichael all jumped in the car and with Stardew driving, they made a clean getaway. Martin S. Ronson glanced out the window at the asteroid as it fell away from him. He saw one of the traffic officers pointing at them in a last attempt to issue a parking ticket. He was not going to be getting his commision today.

With the limo on autopilot, the five of them settled down in the roomy lounge area. There came a noise from the back of the room. They all turned in amazing synchrony. At the back of the room, with a small smirk on her face was Phyllis, the jotaj chief bridesmaid.

'You have no idea how long I've been trying to get those two.'

'Sorry?' replied Stardew, 'who the nazbark are you and why are you on our new stolen limo?'

'My name is Aldebaran-Arcturus-Altair, however I've been going by the name Phyllis for the last eleven years, during my tenure as a spy for the Histapine Horticultural Husbandry Corporation.'

'The Triple H!' interjected Mrs Bambright, excitedly. 'The universe's second biggest horticultural corporation after the Clangwhich Cultivation Compost Conglomerate!'

'Woah! Wait a second, the Quadruple C?!' piped in Martin S. Ronson. 'But they are owned by Troy McClusky, the entrepreneur!'

A morbid voice oozed from one of the chairs.

'I just shot Troy McClusky in the second head with a space-gun.' It was Mr Carmichael.

'Exactly! I had been waiting for the perfect opportunity

to off Reverend McClusky and his arse of a fiancé for some time now, and you guys have just completed the best assassination this side of the Plomantarian Vortex without even knowing it. Plus, you knocked out some traffic cops.'

Stardew chipped in.

'Wait, did you say Reverend McClusky?'

'Yes, it's a little known fact that Troy McClusky was a reverend of the church of the Almost-Virgin Mary. But there's nothing to worry about. That church gets a large payout for each dead reverend and will probably be quite pleased at the news.'

'That's all very well and good, Phyllis,' said Stardew, 'but why have you snuck aboard this limo with us?'

'Well,' she replied, looking sheepish, 'I've been hanging out with Claire and her loser friends for some time now and it was awful. Then after I saw you guys burst in so brilliantly, I thought you looked like a cool crew to join. So I jumped into the limo while you weren't looking, and I wish to hang out with you and join your adventure!'

'Fair enough,' said Martin S. Ronson, 'Take a seat. We're on our way to Corey Carmichael's house, and then off to who knows where!'

Phyllis strapped in, looking very excited for her new adventure. Meanwhile, Mr Carmichael was whispering to Stardew.

'Seems a bit strange doesn't it? I mean, spending 11 years undercover with Claire just to kill Troy McClusky for more market share of the horticulture industry. And anyway, Claire only met Troy 7 years ago! This is all a bit fishy.'

Stardew wasn't listening and just said '*mmm*.' She had been looking at Phyllis' suckers.

*A prime example of a Parking Police Officer*

# Chapter Nein

Corey Carmichael's house was incredibly vast. The space-limousine pulled up to the gate, the ornate gate, the gate so ornate that it made the gates you will have seen going about your life look like a literal pile of shit. Mr Carmichael left the limo and attempted to prise the gate open to allow the vehicle through. Unfortunately, the ornate gate had so much weight that his arm splintered into two pieces. As he screamed, Corey Carmichael exited the limousine.

'Ah, sorry brother. That gate is so hefty that it can only be moved by machinery. It briefly slipped my mind as I watched you attempt to open it there.'

'You knew!' replied Mr Carmichael, through tears of intense pain. 'You knew that the gate would break my arm! Why didn't you say anything?!'

'Yes I knew,' Corey seethed in response. 'Just like you knew what you were doing *twenty years ago*. Anyway, I have an esteemed doctor in my employment, that arm won't stay broken for long.'

Phyllis, Martin S. Ronson, Mrs Bambright and Stardew, the daughter of the king, sat patiently in the space limousine, waiting for the squabbling siblings to calm down. Martin S. Ronson was happy to have a body, after all, that was what he wanted a few chapters ago, but he sort of missed being able to fit in even the smallest places comfortably, like a glove compartment. In reality he wouldn't have wanted to go anywhere near the glove compartment of this space-limo. No way space-José.

Corey whistled, and the gates slowly rotated open around their axes, strong, purposefully, but also a little foreboding. They jutted to a halt, and the space limousine slowly moved forwards down the driveway. This startled our heroes, as nobody was driving.

'Don't worry!' shouted Corey, 'I have a state-of-the-art driverless parking system! It takes control of vehicles and parks them nicely for you. Like a valet that you don't have to tip!'

Martin S. Ronson pondered to himself. *Where on Earth did a terrible stand up comedian get the money for fancy gates and a state-of-the-art, driverless, tipless parking system? And why does he keep giving me that weird look, like he's pondering the dark depths of my soul?* Mrs Bambright and Stardew simultaneously pondered the same thing. Phyllis was staring into the distance, probably thinking about Blue WKD from the hen party. Mr Carmichael was just thinking about how much his arm hurt. Corey Carmichael knew how a terrible stand up comedian got the money for fancy gates and a state-of-the-art driverless parking system, because he was that terrible comedian.

As the limo rolled down the long driveway, it became apparent just how wealthy Corey Carmichael was. The gravelled path was at least a mile (one space-kilometre) long, and was surrounded on both sides by luscious forestry. There were the most rare and beautiful animals and space-animals frolicking between the trees, mainly playing with each other (a couple of xorxagars were fighting a couple of deer, but who can blame them after their history. If we can learn anything from the horrible, torrid history of the xorxagars and the deer, it's that some groups just will never get along).

Phyllis was still thinking about Blue WKD when she saw something out of the corner of her eye. It was a small, glowing orb, strikingly similar to Martin S. Ronson, except this orb did not have a mechanical body. She was about to inform Martin S. Ronson of this, when the orb sped off into the distance and up a small chimney poking out the side of the house. Phyllis started thinking about Blue WKD again, but this time also about Tropical VK.

Eventually, the car arrived at the doors of Corey Carmichael's mega-mansion. That's right, think of a regular mansion, and then multiply it by 10 to the power of 6. That's how big this house was. The mansion was split into three parts – a huge brick cylinder in the centre which rode off seemingly infinitely into the sky, and two brick cubes to either side, each eight stories high. It was a big house. Martin S. Ronson opened his tiny mouth so wide that it looked almost as big as a regular sized mouth.

The limousine parked itself into a parking bay in a car park big enough to house 100 vehicles. There were no other vehicles parked there, which seemed like a waste of a car park, really. Our heroes got out of the limousine and were all overwhelmed by the scale of Corey Carmichael's dwellings.

'Corey…' started Mr Carmichael.

'I know,' interrupted the terrible comedian. 'It is rather much, isn't it?'

'How can you afford this?!'

'How does anyone afford anything?'

Mr Carmichael tried to think of a response through the searing pain of his arm.

'Erm, well they have lots of money…'

'Exactly. Come along, let's head inside and make some copies of that there floppy disk.'

The doors to the mansion were even heavier than the gates we saw before – Mr Carmichael knew better than to break his other arm trying to get them open. Corey let out a sound *just like* a female barn owl's mating call, and the doors flung open. Several male barn owls that looked used to disappointment glanced over from a nearby tree, and didn't even bother to flap over to see what the fuss was about when they saw the doors opening.

Our intrepid travellers walked through the open doorway, intrepidly. The outside of Corey Carmichael's home looked gaudy and expensive, but it paled in comparison to the inside of his home. Every surface was covered in gold. The staircases, the bookcases, the suitcases, everything. The floors, the doors, the stuffed boars and more that were located in the corner of each room were gilded in a thick layer of gold.

Corey Carmichael's esteemed physician was named Dr Goldstein, and had been employed by the comedian based solely on her name, with no attention paid to her credentials. She was also covered in gold.

'Welcome!' shouted the doctor. 'Ah! I see you have a broken arm! Let me attend to that.'

Mr Carmichael walked over to the shining surgeon and showed her his broken limb.

'Ah, a nasty break! It looks to me like you tried to open the gates to the driveway!'

'You're good!' said Mr Carmichael, excitedly. 'Can you fix the damn thing?'

'I sure can!'

And with that, she smacked Mr Carmichael's arm with such force that it broke again in another place.

He screamed, loudly.

Now, if Corey Carmichael had bothered to check the

credentials of his doctor, he would have known that she never actually finished medical school. In fact, she was dismissed after four weeks into her first rotation on the ward after trying to cure a patient's cancer with lemons. Fortunately for Corey Carmichael, a space wizard had cast a spell on him as a child, so he never fell ill or suffered from injury. This was the first time the doctor had needed to prove her worth. She looked around nervously, thinking to herself *come on Goldie, what can you remember about broken arms*? The doctor reached into her doctor's satchel, which she'd been given on her first day of medical school. She pulled out a plaster and tentatively went to place it on the broken arm.

'Now this shouldn't hurt a bit...'

'For goodness sake!' interjected Mrs Bambright, 'A plaster won't do anything, you silly snorkleflart!'

*Rats. I've been rumbled.*

'Is it me or is it warm in here?' croaked Dr Goldstein, sheepishly. She then pretended to faint.

'Oh my!' she cried as she fell.

Nobody believed that she'd actually fainted, mainly due to the fact that she immediately opened one eye to see how people had reacted. She realised what she'd done and closed the eye again, but it was too late.

'Right,' said Mrs Bambright, 'I'm no qualified doctor,

but I've been through enough wars to know how to splint up a broken arm. We'll have to get you to surgery once we've finished our adventures, but this should help you last until we can get to a real doctor. There isn't a space-A&E for space-miles. Corey, do you have any wooden splints?'

'Only golden ones.'

'That will have to do.'

\*\*\*

Phyllis, Martin S. Ronson, Stardew, Mrs Bambright and the Carmichaels were now sat in golden chairs in Corey Carmichael's third best living room (he keeps the second best for royal visitors, and the first best just in case Sting were ever to drop by). Mr Carmichael was nursing his sore, now gilded, arm and Phyllis was thinking about Blue WKD. They were disk-ussing *[Editors note: please don't keep this in]* the floppy disk and the nature of its contents, when Martin S. Ronson heard a familiar sound coming from the mansion's ventilation system.

'Corey,' he started, 'I hate to alarm you, but I think there may be golplorx in your vents. I don't know why they'd end up here, they're usually only found in spacecraft, but if anyone knows how to identify a golplorx, it's me.'

Corey Carmichael's demeanor shifted. He hunched over

slightly, and began to sweat a little.

'And what would you know about golplorx? I know a golplorx when I see one, and I've never seen one in my house.'

'Well, I *am* one!'

It turns out Biffin Bambright's bodies were very deceptive, and Martin S. Ronson was now unrecognisable as a golplorx. The fact he *was* one seemed to have spooked Corey Carmichael, which was not surprising, given the reputation of the species.

'Right, well I'm not having a golplorx in *my* house. Golplorx are scum of the universe. I'm not racist, I just tell it how it is.'

'But he's different!' interjected Stardew. 'He's a nice golplorx!'

'No such thing,' responded Corey. 'The day I meet a nice golplorx is the day hell freezes over, and not space-hell, which is well known for its low temperatures. Good, old fashioned, Catholic hell! Let me take you to the floppy disk reproduction room, and then you can go back to where you came from.'

Corey stood up, and motioned for the others to do the same. He led them out of his third best living room, and into one of the long, winding corridors that built up the network between the rooms of his house. Each corridor was lined with gilded, signed, photos of Sting. He'd never met Sting, but had paid a small fortune for signed memorabilia on space-eBay. One of the signatures was a fake unfortunately, however Corey didn't know, and neither did anyone who came visiting, so for all intents and purposes it didn't really matter. Still, it was, as a fact of the universe, a fake.

After what seemed like hours, and was actually hours (the house was massive), the group arrived at the only door in the whole mansion that was not covered in gold. The room had a massive, almost comically sized padlock on the door, and a sign above the entrance that said 'NO ENTRY! THIS ROOM CONTAINS NOTHING SUSPICIOUS, BUT YOU CAN'T COME IN ANYWAY'.

'NOT THAT ROOM!' screamed Corey Carmichael. 'It's this room, opposite that door.'

Our heroes and Phyllis turned to the room opposite the room that contained nothing suspicious, and Corey Carmichael let them in. The room was actually pretty small in comparison to the other rooms in the house. About thirty floppy-disk drives lined the wall at its far end.

Corey opened a filing cabinet. Inside the cabinet were hundreds and hundreds of blank floppy disks – enough to copy the contents of Martin S. Ronson's disk on to and begin the dissemination process. Corey was getting impatient.

'Well we haven't got all day! Get copying!'

He took Martin S. Ronson's floppy disk and placed it into the master replicator that was connected to the rest of the drives. He pressed a few buttons and stood in front of what looked like a facial recognition camera. A green light blinked and the drive began to whir.

Each main character and Phyllis (who was still working her way towards main character status) took a batch of floppy disks and began to insert them, one by one, into the floppy disk drives. It took them about half an hour, but eventually they had enough copies of the floppy disk to change the course of humanity and space-humanity.

They were exhausted and sweaty, but Corey wasn't having them around for much longer.

'OK, you have your disks, now I think that you should go. And take your smelly golplorx with you!'

He turned to point at Martin S. Ronson, but he was nowhere to be seen. He had detached himself from his beautiful new body and was no longer in the room. Stardew was confused.

'Where the devil is Martin S. Ronson?!'

Martin S. Ronson's interest had been piqued by the room that contained nothing suspicious. He could hear rumblings of a sound he recognised, that had been obviously muffled by soundproofing. Fortunately, all Golplox children learn how to pick locks when they are fresh from the womb, in case they need to access restricted areas of spaceships. He had the door to the room open in seconds.

When he saw what the room contained, he almost fainted. It was the biggest room he'd ever seen in his life. It went back by about a mile from the door that he'd just opened. Crammed into every nook and cranny of that room were small, floating orbs, that looked just like him. The room was full of golplorx.

They weren't just floating about. They were chained to each other in a huge, messed up conga line. Each had a small magnet attached to the bottom of its sphere, which was being manipulated by electrical currents to keep the goplorx moving in formation. At the centre of the room there was a conveyor belt that each magnet was eventually drawn to. That conveyor belt led to a machine labelled *CRISPR*.

There was something dark going on here, and Martin S. Ronson did *not* like the smell of it. He quickly looked up CRISPR on space-wikipedia and found out that it stands for 'Clustered Regularly Interspaced Short Palindromic Repeats'. This didn't clarify anything.

'Oh boy,' he said out loud.

A voice echoed from the doorway.

'I think you mean *'Oh girl,'* you dirty rotten golplorx'. It was Corey Carmichael.

'What do you mea–?'

'–Silence!' Shouted the terrible, racist, and probably sexist comedian. 'Do you really want to know how I made all my billions of space-currency, even though I'm an unsuccessful comedian?'

'What I *want* to know is why you've got so many innocent looking golplorx all chained up in a room which you *specifically* labelled as not being suspicious?! In fact, now that I'm in here, I can see that it *is* highly suspicious!'

'Do you know what CRISPR is, Martin S. Ronson?'

Martin S. Ronson rotated himself from side-to-side, to give the impression that he was shaking his head.

'Well, let me give you a lesson in basic genomic engineering. The CRISPR/Cas system is a prokaryotic immune system that confers resistance to foreign genetic elements such as those present within plasmids and phages that provides a form of acquired immunity. RNA harboring the spacer sequence helps Cas (CRISPR-associated) proteins recognize and cut exogenous DNA. Other RNA-guided Cas proteins cut foreign RNA. CRISPRs are found in approximately 40% of sequenced bacterial genomes and 90% of sequenced archaea. CRISPR is an abbreviation of Clustered Regularly Interspaced Short Palindromic Repeats. The name was minted at a time when the origin and use of the interspacing subsequences were not known. At that time the CRISPRs were described as segments of prokaryotic DNA containing short, repetitive base sequences. In a palindromic repeat, the sequence of nucleotides is the same in both directions. Each repetition is followed by short segments of spacer DNA from previous exposures to foreign DNA (e.g., a virus or plasmid). Small clusters of cas (CRISPR-associated system) genes are located next to CRISPR sequences.'

'Hold on,' interrupted Martin S. Ronson, 'this sounds like it's been copied from Wikipedia!'

'Shut up!' exclaimed Corey. 'I can use this CRISPR machine to mutate the DNA of any living creature as I see fit. I made my vast fortune through the ingenious application of this little box. I've taken millions of golplorx from their homeplanet of Golplorxainia!'

'Golplorxainia! Why, that's just a myth, a legend, an old *gölplórx* tale from long ago. It doesn't actually exist!'

'No, it doesn't exist, because I blew it up!' cried the worst of the Carmichael twins. Martin S. Ronson produced a look of terror from his face. Corey Carmichael continued.

'I blew it up many years ago, when I was a young and handsome man. I brought the golplorx here to my mansion...'

'Wait, how did you have the mansion already if you hadn't yet made your fortune?'

'SILENCE!' Corey shouted again. 'I brought the

golplorx here, and one by one I genetically altered their DNA to give them a crazed desire to mass produce, infect and takeover spaceships. Once they have full control of a spaceship, they bring it here to me where I refurbish it and sell it off for many space-pounds'.

Martin S. Ronson couldn't believe what he had just heard.

'I can't believe what I've just heard!' he said. 'You are a sick man Mr Carmichael, and to think, your brother is such a nice alien. Although his driving is appalling.'

'He hasn't told you what happened between us 20 years ago, has he?'

'No he hasn't, but whatever it was, it can't be as bad as destroying a planet, enslaving a whole species, altering their DNA and setting them upon innocent spaceships to gain a vast fortune of space-euros!'

'Well, I would suggest you ask him about that. However, it's now time for your DNA to be altered, your memory to be erased, and for my money to continue flowing in!'

Corey Carmichael grabbed Martin S. Ronson and strapped him down onto the conveyor belt of the CRISPR machine. Martin S. Ronson screamed.

'What are you doing? LET GO OF ME!'

'I literally just explained to you what I'm doing, and no!'

It was too late for pleads and conversation. Martin S.

Ronson was strapped down, and Corey Carmichael pulled a comically large lever which had the word 'GO' written above it.

A loud humming noise started sounding and some lights began to flash, greens, blues and one colour unrecognisable to the human eye, but pretty normal to all aliens, also this is a book and we couldn't afford colour printing, so it really doesn't matter. Corey chuckled to himself. He was very proud of his invention, and was very pleased to have captured an unruly golplorx so easily.

Inside the machine, Martin S. Ronson was having a horrible time. He was being thrown this way and that way and those ways and these ways. He was stretched and squashed and massaged (which was actually quite nice), but then hit right in the goolies (which was not). He felt like Augustus Gloop going up the chocolate chute, and he feared that he was going to end up the same way as all the children from Charlie and the Chocolate Factory – dead.

Colours were swirling all around him, and in and out of him. He saw two streams of DNA float above his head, twisting and turning in the light, spewing out various letters: Gs, As, Cs and Ts. The occasional X would appear, but then it would rotate in a blur, and our distressed and inconvenienced hero would realise it was just a lowercase T, which didn't make *any* sense, unlike the rest of this book.

Suddenly, a speaker sounded.

'DNA MUTATION! DNA MUTATION! DNA MUTATION!' said a classic robotic voice.

'What?!' shouted Corey, who had been enjoying the whole thing because he was not a nice guy. 'DNA mutation? How can that be?! Golplorx DNA never mutates in the wild, that was what made all this CRISPR stuff quite easy.'

Why was it that Martin S. Ronson had been so very different from all the other golplorx on Captain Morf's ship? Well, the clue is in what the classic robotic voice just said.

Martin S. Ronson flew straight out the end of the CRISPR machine, and whacked a massive blow to Corey's confused face, shouting his favourite line of this whole novel:

'Mutate *this*, bitch!'

Corey stumbled backwards towards the machine, clutching a hand to his poorly face. He regained his balance.

'Get your paws off me, you damn, dirty golplorx!'

He ran towards Martin S. Ronson at full pace, grabbed him, and threw him with all his might at the wall. Our hero slid down the wall slowly, ending up in a heap of small floating orb at the bottom.

Martin S. Ronson was dizzy, and everything was shifting in his eyesight. Corey strolled over to him with a disgusting swagger.

'Looks like your time is up. I should have killed you as soon as I realised that you were a golplorx, but I was cocky and wanted to turn you into a ship-stealing minion. However, I was wrong about you. You're stronger than the other golplorx, and a strong golplorx is dangerous. You deserve death.'

Corey lifted his massive boots.

'And for that reason I am going to stamp on you right now!'

SMASH! Something shattered on the back of Corey Carmichael's head. Martin S. Ronson looked up. Everything was still spinning in a haze, but was starting to come back together again. He could make out some kind of blue liquid trickling down Corey's face as he collapsed to the floor next to him.

The unmistakable and unbelievable smell of a worryingly bright alcopop was music to his little alien ears. Behind Corey's limp body appeared the shape of Phyllis. Martin S. Ronson had never noticed how blue her eyes were, the same stunning shade as a 700ml bottle of WKD.

The others all rushed in afterwards.

'Oh my! What's happened here?' exclaimed Mr Carmichael, the more noble and less evil of the two Carmichael twins, despite the incident of 20 years previously.

'I'm sorry Mr Carmichael,' replied Phyllis, 'I smashed a bottle of WKD Blue over your brother's head. He was trying to CRISPR Martin S. Ronson and turn him into a spaceship hungry monster like what everyone thinks he is. I know how important family is to people, I've seen *Home Alone 2*! All this time I've spent thinking about WKD I was actually working out how effective it would be at killing someone, it's just part of my learning on the job.'

Obviously, no one had known what Phyllis had been thinking about, but it didn't really matter.

Mrs Bambright couldn't help himself.

'CRISPR is not a verb, is it? In fact I'm not sure any of this works in the way Corey Carmichael just described.' Everyone ignored him, although he was right, giving Mrs Bambright a feeling of self doubt that this/these author(s) is/are very used to.

'Phyllis my dear,' replied Mr Carmichael in his grandad voice, 'family is important. However, when mass enslavery of an entire species is involved simply to improve the demand for your spaceship refurbishing business, you've just got to realise my brother is a twat. Now, you've done very well at learning on the job my dear, but Corey is not actually dead, just unconscious. I guess that if you'd used a prosecco bottle he would have died, but that's by the by. You did good. Now, let's tie him up.'

This comment by Mr Carmichael, although well meant, was pretty patronising, but as we've said before he was old and had fought in the space war on all twelve sides. Therefore, he was forgiven for a lot of things.

Stardew picked up the unconscious Corey Carmichael and carried him over to a chair, where she and Mrs Bambright tied him up with a length of glowing orange space-rope.

'Martin S. Ronson,' said Stardew, 'would you care to do the honours?' She was pointing towards a huge lever with a sign above it that said *Freedom*. It was the lever that would release the magnets restraining all the golplorx in the room. Martin S. Ronson glided over and pulled on the lever. Nothing happened. The group heard a moan from behind them, and all turned in unison to see Corey Carmichael, who had regained consciousness.

'You idiots, why would I have put a big freedom lever on the wall? That was only there to taunt the golplorx and get them all riled up. It helps to CRISPR them more quickly.'

Mrs Bambright sighed and was about to question the science of Corey Carmichael's methods, when Stardew piped up.

'Don't worry! I've found the plug.' She pulled on the cable and the big yellow plug at the end popped out of a socket on the wall. The hum of the motor which had been in the background the whole time came to a stop, and then the sound of thousands upon millions of tiny little shackles opening filled the room. It was a taste of victory for Martin S. Ronson, and it tasted delicious and not at all CRISPR-y (!).

Corey Carmichael lifted his pounding head, only to see the mass of golplorx flying towards him with immense power.

Our band of unlikely heroes (including Phyllis. Yes, Phyllis!) turned and walked out the door of the room without looking back to witness Corey's fate. Stardew grabbed the keys to the house and the limo off the side, and placed them into her pocket. Mrs Bambright had a large sack over his shoulder full of brand spanking new floppy disks, which contained the most powerfully important information that had ever existed.

As the door closed, Martin S. Ronson turned to Mr Carmichael.

'Mr Carmichael, can you tell me what you did twenty years ago?'

'The path of light and wisdom is a long road, dear Martin S. Ronson. Do not let your better judgement cast dark shadows on the remains of the day. I'm afraid I will not tell you now...' replied Mr Carmichael, '...but one day you will find out.'

Mr Carmichael was very wise.

As for the doctor, she was never seen again by our crew, but she took some of Corey's money and enrolled on a dentistry course at King's College on the planet Tenalpekaf in the Palfmub system. We wish her the best of luck.

*[Editor's note: Goldstein has since failed the dentistry course for attempting to treat every ailment with garlic.]*

\*\*\*

Once in the space-limo, everyone went for a well earned nap. Upon waking, Martin S. Ronson floated through into the cockpit to find Mr Carmichael and Stardew talking. Mr Carmichael's wise words and the adventures in the mansion had affected the golplorx greatly, and he had decided to stop using his new body and try to live proudly in his true golplorx skin. Mrs Bambright was a bit miffed though because he'd spent ages making it.

'Have you worked out where we should be headed next?' said Martin S. Ronson.

'Well,' replied Mr Carmichael, 'as a matter of fact we have. We are going to make a direct course for the Tralmordian System.'

'The Tralmordian System? Cool!' shouted Martin S. Ronson. 'They've got an amusement park right?'

'Exactly,' replied Stardew, 'they've got the greatest theme park this side of the space-equator, *Screaming Sam's Rickety Rocking Party Park*!'

Mrs Bambright popped his cylindrical head round the corner.

'Woah, woah, woah. What possible need do we have to go to *S.S.R.R.P.P.*? I thought we were part of some crazy adventure to do with that floppy disk and saving the universe?'

He sounded slightly disappointed, but was also a bit happy because he'd always wanted to go to *S.S.R.R.P.P.* since he was a little girl.

'We are,' snorted Stardew. 'Do you know what extra special calendar event is in their events calendar?'

Mrs Bambright shook his head.

'It's the universe's greatest interplanetary bicentennial basketball championship final, and on the other side of the park, the EU (European Universe) is deciding whether or not to let Tralmax-Seven into the customs union, after it allowed the Bizza-Bizza-Bizza's second moon Kiylolo in last year. All of the galaxy's media is going to be there. Can you think of a better place to show the universe this floppy disk?'

Mrs Bambright shook his head again

'Well then,' said Stardew. 'Mr Carmichael, get that good

arm into gear! To the Tralmordian System!'

'Wait, how long is it going to take us to get there?' asked Martin S. Ronson.

'I think it's about four months.'

'Four months?! Wait is that, Diligord-4 months?'

'Yes of course,' replied Stardew, wanting to get going as soon as possible.

'And what's the rotatory code for Diligord-4?' said Martin S. Ronson.

'Eugh, it's about 29B I think.'

'Well, 29B times the star sign of the Tramoldian System, plus seven seconds to account for space time colours... and three extra arcminutes because of vortex calculus. Oh, I make that only two days. Excellent!'

As a space infant yourself, you would be forgiven (but only just) for thinking that the Intergalactic Federation of the Universe would have come up with some kind of universal clock or way of telling time, probably based on time passed since the big bang. Unfortunately, they hadn't, and these kinds of conversations were rife throughout the galaxy, wasting everyone's time (no matter how it was measured).

Stardew was tired of this nonsense, as I'm sure you are.

'Right, well that's better. Two Tralmodian days to go.' She then repeated what she'd said earlier as she didn't think anyone had heard her the first time.

'Well then,' said Stardew. 'Mr Carmichael, get that good arm into gear! To the Tralmordian System!'

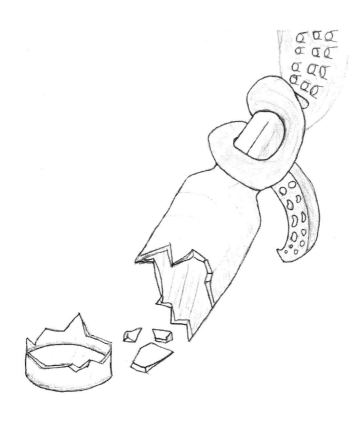

*Phyllis steps up*

# Chapter – . –.

On a plain, very small, yet luscious planet that held many, many beautiful vistas stood two wilderwrawn – great hulking beasts covered in short, deadly sharp spines. They were gentle creatures with simple lives, that failed to impact heavily at all upon the twisting and turning of life upon the planet. Once in a blue moon, which was twice a month, a wandering bansnark would stroll into their territory looking for food and would be chased away, but this was as close to an impression upon the planet that these two creatures would get to.

They mostly just shuffled around like elderly people, snuffling up truffles with their muffles, rarely engaging in any kind of kerfuffle, and definitely having no wider understanding of the large parliamentary reshuffle on the planet some 180 million km away (112 million miles-ish) (180 million space-miles).

One feature of these animals that would be of some concern to the likes of us is that they had evolved to emit a constant sound – the result of an irregularly twisted oesophagus. This sound would ebb and flow, changing persistently. Curiously, it resembles identically the voice of Sir Elton John, and anyone with a whim for the piano/rocket/glasses man would recognise the voice immediately. They would also be very confused as to why they could hear such a sound, constantly talking incoherently about nothing, on a plain on a small and luscious planet. However, possibly fortunately for them, all of the inhabitants of this planet were deaf, or rather they did not have auditory organs at all.

The planet in question was one which is often termed a 'Class 67' planet, meaning it had not yet evolved to a state of 'civilisation', and no one could be bothered to go along to help it because there was an exceptionally good cinema and shopping planet nearby, which people preferred to go to if they are were that local area.

The weather on this planet was mostly calm with rain being fairly regular on Wednesdays. Today was a Friday, which made the wilderwrawn quite happy as they looked forward to the weekend. A light drizzle had been falling all afternoon, which concerned them slightly. By around 5:34pm, the light drizzle had riled up into what could only be described as 'pissing it down', and by 8:03pm there was a medium size tornado whizzing around the planet, lifting up cows, sheds and other such things one would expect to see in a tornado.

Suddenly and quite instantly, a huge lightning bolt struck right through the core of the tornado. It was a catastrophic event that would have sounded gargantuan and terrifying if anybody there had had ears. It also looked totally nutso. For a split second the lightning strike took the perfect shape of a spoon, which I think we will all agree is the perfect shape.

The wilderwrawn sprung up onto their back legs, screaming furiously at the sky in Elton's voice:

'Duchess Constabularly!'

Just to confirm, the wilderwrawn have no concept of the English language, but just make the noises.

Following the lightning strike the tornado fell away, the storm subsided, and the wilderwrawn put their umbrellas down (they had been holding umbrellas).

Lying at what had been the base of the tornado was a solitary figure. There was a quick, sharp intake of breath as the individual lifted its head up violently. Although the creatures on the planet had never witnessed anything resembling this shape, they knew instantly that they were viewing the most beautiful, handsome and stunning alien that they would ever view in their lives. The figure's body and facial features were so well defined that by just holding some graphite and standing near some paper, the photons from a strong enough light would get all agitated and then refract, reflect and distract themselves into the most beautiful portrait you have ever seen. His face seemed to emit a glow. Aliens would burst into tears of joy and/or fear at viewing his face, and if you placed a delicate glass rose nearby it would shatter in pure satisfaction at the sight. In other words, he was hot to trot.

The teleportation that this character had undergone had

transformed him visually into this spectacular being. He used to be a gargoyley demon who carried soup to his master. Furthermore, and this next fact had only been noticed by the individual, the effects of the lightning and teleportation had caused him to not only to become beautiful, but also inadvertently shit himself. This was as uncomfortable as you would expect, but he had work to do.

He glanced around, noticing for the first time that the two alien creatures had assembled around him, with a look of awe upon their faces. He stared at the wilderwrawn and knew he needed to tame the creatures. He casually approached the larger of the two and then jumped enthusiastically onto its back. He ignored the constant blabbing of the creature, although he somehow recognised the voice, and used the surge of energy that he had still running through his fingers from the tornado and lightning to zap the creature.

At once the wilderwrawn began to lift into the air. This was an incredible experience for the creature who spent almost every day just wandering around eating. The grass surrounding the event was shaking violently due to the increase in powerful activity that it was not used to. The other wilderwrawn glanced up at its lifelong friend and slowly came to the realisation that it was drifting away and that it may never see it again. A single tear slipped down the wilderwrawn's face.

As the two new accomplices floated gradually upward, the handsome individual thought to himself '*Wow, I had no idea what I was doing for a second there, but it seems to be working out fine*'.

As they flew through the air, he thanked the wilderwrawn for being so obliging and agreeing to help him.

'Thank you for being so obliging and agreeing to help me. I think I will name you Anihcamxesued, the traditional name of my ancestors, but I will call you Deus for short. My name is Gorgol, and by the way, I am the bad guy.'

Deus the wilderwrawn was deaf, so didn't hear a word of that, and had no idea that he was in the vicinity of the bad guy, never mind accidentally being of service to him. Although deaf, Deus the wilderwrawn could smell, and something strange he did sniff. The air that surrounded them had a sickly, sweet, aroma, much like the air surrounding a candy floss stall at a parade. This smell was actually coming from Gorgol's defecation, that had been whipped up by the twister and flung into the poor wilderwrawn's nostrils.

This was no regular poo, unfortunately. Back in the kitchen of the black and dark and grim place, Gorgol had been sampling his delicious soup with the Spoon of Valaxion, making sure it was as tasty as possible for the Master. Unfortunately for Deus, this causes the user's waste products to mutate the brain of any unfortunate soul who may smell it, becoming a loyal servant to the defecator. Deus the Wilderwrawn had no interest in uniting the spheres, or in helping Gorgol's master to achieve their immortal goal, but by this point it was too late. The shit was in his nose, and the evil was taking over.

Gorgol then did something which seems rather drastic, but turned out to be quite clever. He grabbed the Spoon of Valaxion from the pocket of his shitty trousers, and rammed it into the skull of the wilderwrawn. This of course caused the once galliant beast to fall back to the ground at speed. For a moment, the other wilderwrawn was pleased because it thought it may see its friend again. Gorgol managed to jump off at the perfect time, did a nice little roll, and then stood up (he didn't adjust his cufflinks like that *idiot* James Bond does in Skyfall.)

The impact formed a crater a space-kilometre deep. Out of the skull of Deus, a single green stem shot up. It grew slowly at first, but then the pace quickened. Shortly, the crater was covered in green shrubbery. A seductive rumbling occured and from the greenery a large tower began to grow. The walls of the tower were a yellowy white. A keen eyed viewer would realise they were the pure, shimmering bones of the majestic creature.

You may think that it makes no sense for a massive tower to grow out of the skull of an alien creature who'd just been bashed to death with a spoon, but if this were a film (which it may well be one day) you would instead be amazed at the incredible special effects, and then even more amazed when you find that we never actually used special effects, but just played a video of the demolition of a tower in reverse. The tower was brilliant and bold. Like Orthanc and Baradur in the Lord of the Rings it was scary and menacing, but like Fawlty Towers it was white and had rats.

As the tower grew out of the crater, Gorgol grabbed hold and was lifted up with it. He then placed his perfect buttocks on the newly grown bone throne. He was waiting for the one and only day in the next millenium that the spheres could be united.

That day just so happened to coincide with two other events. A basketball final and an EU customs union vote. And this new tower just so happened to be placed at the site of the 'world' famous *Screaming Sam's Rickety Rocking Party Park*. It would only be 970 years until it was built.

Gorgol had a lot to prepare. His first job was making some new trousers.

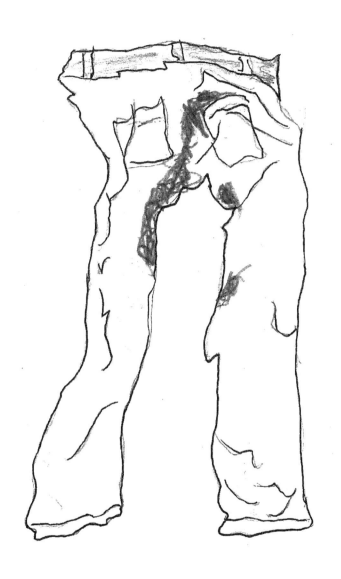

*Defecation, defecation, defecation*

# Chapter ♯

The Tralmordian system was a lot further away than Mr Carmichael remembered. Martin S. Ronson had forgotten to carry a two when he was doing his space-time calculations earlier, and it was actually quite the journey. Mr Carmichael had been to *S.S.R.R.P.P.* once before as a young boy, long before work on their flagship rollercoaster *Smash Mouth's All Star Wild Ride* had even started. One of his favourite childhood memories was of his young feet gracing the wooden boards of the Wild West area, complete with animatronic cowboys and real indians.

The history of the wild west had been long malformed over millenia. Mr Carmichael's boyhood memories were of tall, half-cow-half-aliens, a kind of bovine centaur, and of surprisingly authentic South Indian curries, from the region of Kerala. He could almost smell it now, and began to water at the mouth. If only the space-limousine could enter warp speed!

Stardew was reading a space-celebrity magazine that had been left in the limousine by its previous occupants. Space-celebrity magazines are nothing like the celebrity magazines you may be accustomed to on Earth. There is no concept of paparazzi outside of our home planet – and in fact, the first thing that inhabitants of the universe's other planets did when they made contact with us was to give us a right telling off that we didn't have more respect for privacy. The second thing they did was make Piers Morgan swallow mobile phones until he had a bellyache, and asked if he understood the irony. He didn't know what irony meant. Space-celebrity magazines, devoid of secretly taken photographs and untrue gossip, are just crosswords where the answer to every riddle is 'Tom Hanks'.

Martin S. Ronson was now back in his beautiful new body. This was following a rather heated and emotionally charged conversation with Mrs Bambright which is available on disk two of your HD-DVD. He was now engaged in a game of rock-paper-scissors with Phyllis. Fortunately for Martin S. Ronson, his body came equipped with an actual rock, an actual piece of paper and an actual pair of scissors. Phyllis had to use her left sucker, which she wasn't able to maneuver into any of the aforementioned objects, so was no match for the little orb. She was having a good time bonding with her new friend, however, and didn't mind that she'd lost 82 games in a row.

Mrs Bambright had found the stash of champagne that was still on ice in the back of the limo. He'd necked a couple of bottles already and was feeling very snoozy. He curled up into a ball like a cat, and began to snore. He dreamt of a simpler time, before he'd met the little orb and his floppy disk, and tried to decide whether it was better or worse than the situation he found himself in now.

The ship's Universal Positioning System estimated that there were still fourteen hours of the journey left before our heroes arrived at *S.S.R.R.P.P.*, and everyone was starting to get bored and restless.

'I am so bored!' yawned Stardew, who had figured out that the answer to every column and every row of the crossword was going to be 'Tom Hanks', which completely killed the fun of it. 'What can we do to pass the time?'

Mr Carmichael nodded in agreement.

'We're in a luxury space-limousine, there must be a TV or something back there!'

'Good shout. I'll see if I can find a remote'.

She felt down the sides of all of the space-cushions, and lo and behold, she found a remote control. She pressed the 'on' button, and, lo and behold again, a well concealed television burst into life on the inner roof of the limousine. It was playing an advert for toothpaste.

'Jackpot,' said Stardew.

'Are there any good films?' asked Martin S. Ronson, who was beginning to tire of flexing his scissors. '*Hot Tub Time Machine 2*, perhaps?'

*Hot Tub Time Machine 2* had been panned by critics upon its release many, many years previously, but had stood the test of time and was now regarded as one of mankind's greatest artistic achievements, much like Weezer's

*Pinkerton* or *The Bible*.

'I'll have a look,' replied Stardew, but she couldn't see the *Hot Tub Time Machine 2* button that was standard across all remote controls of the era. She sighed, and pressed the next best thing, which was a circular button containing a question mark.

The button had barely begun depressing from its fully pressed state when the toothpaste advert screeched to a halt and the screen was replaced with a close up of the recently deceased Troy McClusky's second face. Mr Carmichael shivered. Despite the fact he joked about blowing the reverend's second head to smithereens at the time, he'd actually been quite affected by the encounter, and seeing the second head fully intact on screen was making him feel guilty. He closed his eyes and tutted to himself.

'Oh yes,' said Phyllis, 'we had to watch a disgusting, saccharine, lovey-dovey video from the reverend on our way to the comedy club. I think this is the end of it. Press the play button, I think he taped over an episode of *Mothers of Tsars Dance with the Stars*. There should still be most of the episode left on the tape!' Martin S. Ronson looked excited by the prospect of seeing his favourite TV show.

'Jackpot!'

Stardew pressed play. The tape continued on, the reverend still in focus. He appeared to reach for the video camera's stop button, but didn't press it properly. His attitude changed completely, and it was obvious that he thought he was no longer being recorded, a bit like Gordon Brown in 2010 when he called that bigoted woman a bigot.

'Bloody hell. I'd rather an old man shot my second head off than marry that woman.'

Mr Carmichael smiled slightly.

Still on the screen, the Reverend Troy McClusky turned his back to the camera and powered up his personal computer, which was in the frame of the video. He took something down from the shelf above the computer, and slotted it into an archaic looking drive that was on the desk next to it. Martin S. Ronson's eyes widened.

'Is that a…'

He couldn't finish his sentence. Stardew was just as wide mouthed.

'Oh my god. It is.'

Everybody except the sleeping Mrs Bambright was intensely focused on the screen now. They all saw the Reverend Troy McClusky push a floppy disk into his floppy disk drive, and begin to chant.

*'Gorgol, awake.*
*Awake, sweet Gorgol.*
*The travellers shall land atop your resting head soon'*

As he finished his chant, the screen burst into colour. Our heroes gasped as one. His screen was ablaze with the contents of the floppy disk they had just made so many copies of.

'What the hell is going on?!' exclaimed Martin S. Ronson. Mr Carmichael shook his head.

'I don't know, but I don't like the look of it one bit. As excited as I am to walk the boards of the wild west once more, maybe we should steer clear of *S.S.R.R.P.P.* for a while.'

He stepped over to the space-limousine's console and opened up the coordinates menu.

'Odd…'

'What's up?' asked Stardew.

'The console… it's frozen. I can't change our coordinates. This is very strange. I'll try to find the manual override button'.

He dug around in the wires underneath the console.

'Oh no. Oh no, oh no, oh no.'

He found where the manual override was supposed to be. But the button had been torn out and removed. In its place was a photograph. He reached inside and took the photograph out.

'What the hell?!'

'What is it?' asked Martin S. Ronson.

'It's a picture of *Smash Mouth's All Star Wild Ride*. And there's a note on the back.'

'What does it say?'

Mr Carmichael gulped.

'It says… *Tell Gorgol that I love him.*'

'Who the *hell* is this Gorgol character?' asked Phyllis.

'I have no idea,' replied Mr Carmichael, 'but I can't change our coordinates. I have a feeling we're going to be meeting him pretty soon.'

Everybody took a seat and sat in silence for a while. *Mothers of Tsars Dance with the Stars* had started on the television screen, but now not even Martin S. Ronson was interested.

\*\*\*

The space-limousine entered the Tralmordian system, and joined a line of vehicles awaiting entry. It was an incredibly busy day and the vehicles were full of basketball players and fans, and European diplomats. Mr Carmichael noticed something that gave him a little hope that they wouldn't have to meet this Gorgol fellow today after all.

'They're inspecting everybody's car parking tickets! Maybe they'll turn us away!'

'I hope so,' replied Martin S. Ronson, 'I have a really bad

feeling about this Gorgol character. All I wanted to do was disseminate a little universe-shattering information, and now I might have to defeat some sort of nemesis instead!'

The space limousine rolled up to a floating car park barrier. The barrier was just for show, as in space you can travel in three dimensions and easily go underneath or over the top of it, but if you tried such a manoeuvre you'd be pulled in by a giant magnet and flung back into space by a catapult. The space-limousine made it to the barrier, and a small alien wearing a fancy hat appeared at the driver's window. Mr Carmichael rolled this window down.

'Hello there, have you got a car parking pass today, sir?' the alien asked him.

'Ah. I'm afraid I don't. I suppose we'll be catapulted back into space then?'

'Hmm. Let me speak to my manager.'

The alien in the fancy hat turned around and made a hand gesture to his manager. On Earth, it's a very rude hand gesture, but in the Tralmordian System it purely means 'come over here and see if this car is allowed into the car park'. The manager arrived at Mr Carmichael's window.

'I am so sorry Reverend!' said the manager, apologetically. 'Your car has been booked into the system well in advance, and you should have been transported automatically into the fast lane. Our system is a little on the fritz right now what with all of this traffic and it must have misread your space-licence plate! Ever so sorry!'

Mr Carmichael gulped.

'Ah, I'm not the Reverend!' he replied.

'Well who are you then? If you're not with the Reverend, then I'll have to take you down to the cells while we figure out why you have his car!'

Rats. If they had to go into the park, Mr Carmichael thought it would be better to be a free alien than trapped in a cell, unable to do anything. They *had* stolen the car, and he didn't want to raise any suspicions.

'No, no! This is his car. He's asleep in the back, curled up like a cat. Had a little too much champagne.'

The manager looked at the sleeping Mrs Bambright.

'He looked thinner in his photo. Never mind! Open the barrier!'

And with that, the barrier opened, and the space-limousine began to descend to the surface, where a space in the car park between two members of the Harlem Solar-System-Trotters was available and waiting. It landed. The doors opened. Stardew shook Mrs Bambright awake.

Bleary eyed, he exited the space-limousine first, unaware of the peril they now found themselves in. The manager was stood next to the car, ready to greet them.

'Reverend!' he started. 'How are you today?'

'Reverend?' replied Mrs Bambright. 'What are you talking…'

Mr Carmichael had swiftly exited the car and gave Mrs Bambright an elbow in the ribs.

'Ha ha ha! Great joke, Reverend. A little too much champagne again!' Mrs Bambright looked confused, but figured he should play along and ask questions later.

'Yes! It is me, the Reverend. Thank you for greeting me! We must carry on now!'

'Where are you off to now?' asked the manager. Mr Carmichael took the lead.

'Just headed to *S.S.R.R.P.P.* first! We fancy a delicious curry in the wild west section after all of that travelling!'

'Excellent choice!' replied the manager. He pointed to the floor. 'If you follow this green line all the way through the entrance, past the land of microwaves, and over the fizzy chocolate lake, the pleasure garden and the rampant missile range, you'll make it to the wild west section! And there are a few excellent specials on today I'm told.'

'Fantastic,' replied Mrs Bambright, trying to deflect as much suspicion as possible, although he was unsure at what they were being supposed of. 'I do enjoy a curry. Well, let's get moving!'

The manager tipped his hat and went back to his post.

'What the devil is going on?' Mrs Bambright asked Mr

Carmichael.

'I'll tell you over a curry.'

The group strolled onwards through the park. Martin S. Ronson was continually amazed by all the amazing things that he saw. You may be used to Thorpe Park, Alton Towers or even, though less likely, Chessington World of Adventures. These are nothing compared to *S.S.R.R.P.P.* The rides here are just *nuts*. One of them, the Spiny Rocket Race Ride actually alters your perception of race and makes everyone you look at for the hour following the ride all one alien race of your choosing. This was a malfunction of the ride when it first happened, but the designers decided to just go with it, and everyone was bloody pleased about it.

'Oh my,' exclaimed Martin S. Ronson, 'I've never seen a place as incredible as this.'

'Yeah buddy,' replied Mrs Bambright, slurping a slush puppy he'd brought from somewhere on the way, 'I've been wanting to come here for such a long time. When I was growing up my family weren't very well off, and my mother always promised she'd take me and my siblings here when they next had a 'kids-go-free' promotion in the cereal. It took me many years to realise that from that day onward we only ever had toast for breakfast.'

Martin S. Ronson looked down at his shoes in a sad way.

'Wow Mrs Bambright, that's very sad and really gives

your character even more depth that we haven't previously seen. I'll tell you what, when this whole space ordeal is over we'll bring you and your siblings here for that day out, with or without a voucher!'

'Gee, Martin S. Ronson, you're a real pal. But my siblings lived on Diligord-4, and therefore died when the planet exploded.'

'Wow,' replied Martin S. Ronson, feeling very sad now and not quite putting two and two together to think about how Stardew had effectively murdered them by blowing up the planet. Unbeknown to either of them, Mrs Bambright's siblings, Mr Wamwright and Miss Samwright, were alive and well and had escaped the doomed planet in the moments before its destruction (in Mrs Bambright's space-religion, siblings share a first name – in this case Biffin – but have rhyming surnames).

They carried on through the park and eventually made it to *Chief Thunderous River's House of Spice*. It was still a popular eating spot even after all these years, and for a moment it looked as if they wouldn't be able to get a table. Fortunately, an extended family of jotaj tourists finished their mango lassis and settled their bill (no tip) as our heroes closed the door behind them. An Indian man came to the door to greet them.

'Hello travellers, and welcome to *Chief Thunderous*

*River's House of Spice*! We have the finest authentic curries this side of the Tralmordian System! Please give me a second to hose down the table after that extended jotaji family.'

As a jojaj herself, Phyllis was slightly embarrassed to be associated with the messy tourists, and hoped that the others wouldn't judge her. They weren't judging her. Martin S. Ronson asked to see the menu.

'May I see the menu? I think my new body may have a gluten intolerance but I'm not sure.'

Mrs Bambright took offence to this.

'Are you trying to say I introduced a gluten intolerance into your new body?! In twenty years of body shopping I'm yet to produce anything other than the perfect vessel.'

'Oh, no, sorry... I didn't mean to offend you. I'm sure it's nothing.' Martin S. Ronson decided to slyly order a gluten-free meal anyway, to avoid upsetting his friend. In fact, the spacesuit that Biffin had used as the basis for Martin S. Ronson's new body didn't interact pleasantly with gluten, and he had missed the warning about this on the label underneath the left shoe. Also, he had previously introduced many intolerances into bodies he'd previously built, but they were so severe that the new owners had died before they could complain.

Mrs Bambright huffed, a little miffed at Martin S.

Ronson's apparent lack of faith in his handiwork. Usually he'd sulk for a couple of hours at this sort of thing, but he knew that there were bigger fish to fry right now. He leaned in to Mr Carmichael, who had just taken a bite of a poppadom that he had dipped in lime pickle.

'Mr Carmichael, what was all of that 'Reverend' business earlier? I was ruddy confused!'

'You missed a whole thing while you were having your booze snooze, Mrs Bambright!' he replied. 'It turns out that the Reverend Troy McClusky *wanted* us to kill him and steal his vehicle, and had pre-booked us a parking space at this very theme park.'

Mrs Bambright huffed again.

'My old friend, that's impossible!'

'We haven't known each other that long!'

'No, but you *are* old!'

The whole table burst out in laughter.

'Anyway,' Mrs Bambright continued, 'we made the decision to come here ourselves! It was Stardew's idea! How could the reverend have possibly known that we were going to head to the Tralmordian System?!'

Stardew paused.

'Wait a second, did you say that *I* made the suggestion to come here?'

Mrs Bambright nodded.

'Yeah, you did. I remember it very clearly. You said that we should come to the *S.S.R.R.P.P.* and hand out the floppy disks, as it's the basketball championship finals, and the EU summit all on the the same day.'

Stardew looked confused.

'I don't remember saying any such a thing. I had no idea any of that was going on before we arrived here! The last thing I remember before we set off was Mr Carmichael shooting Troy McClusky's second head off, and a little piece of his skull landed on my hand.'

A bottle of Blue WKD smashed on the floor. Everybody turned to Phyllis.

'Uh oh.'

'What, Phyllis?' Stardew said.

'I dropped my WKD! Sorry, I wasn't listening. What did you say?'

'I *said* the last thing I remember before we set off here was Mr Carmichael shooting Troy McClusky's second head off, and a little piece of his skull landed on my hand.'

'Uh oh.'

'What, Phyllis?' Stardew said.

'Did it embed into your hand and disappear in the blink of an eye?'

Stardew gulped and blinked her eyes.

'Yes, yes it did. Why? What's happened, Phyllis?'

Phyllis sighed.

'Have you heard of the Two-headed Manchipod?'

Stardew shook her head,

'I can't say I have to be honest. Please, do tell me more.'

'Well, that's the kind of alien Troy McClusky was. When a Two-Headed Manchipod dies, it is able to transmit its last thoughts to somebody else before death, by embedding a part of its body inside them. You must have got that piece of his second skull inside your hand just before the life exited his body.'

'Holy shit,' swore Stardew.

'The thing is, while you are speaking the last thoughts of the Manchipod, you are unable to form memories. Most people are prepared and write it down, or make sure somebody else is present too. Troy McClusky must have realised he was about to die, and made sure his last thoughts were going to lead us here.'

Martin S. Ronson piped up.

'I'm sorry, but it can't have been a coincidence that Stardew ended up with that little piece of Reverend skull in her hand. We all saw the video! He had a copy of the floppy disk!'

'What?!' shouted Mrs Bambright.

'Yeah! We all saw! Except you, you were having a nap.'

'I can't explain that,' said Phyllis, 'but I have a feeling

that we're going to find out a lot more once this Gorgol fellow makes an appearance. I must say, I have no idea what to expect. The dramatic suspense is amazing.'

The waiter had arrived back at the table.

'Hello everyone! Have you all had a chance to look at the menu?'

'Yes,' replied Mr Carmichael. 'We're all going to have a Chicken Tikka Masala, just like the Indians did before going head to head with the cowboys!' Martin S. Ronson wanted to check if it was gluten free, but decided he'd rather upset his digestive system than Mrs Bambright again.

'Fantastic. I'll take your orders to the chef now. Would you like any more poppadoms?'

Mr Carmichael shook his head.

'Very well.' The waiter turned and left the table. He continued through a door back to the kitchen. He walked past the chef and dropped the piece of paper containing the order for our heroes' table on the work bench next to her. He continued past the alien who washed the dishes, and pushed open another door, which lead to a metallic spiral staircase. He took the first step, and then the next, and then the third, he was walking down the stairs normally. He got to the bottom step, and there was yet another door that he went through. He pushed this one open, and entered another room.

This was an *incredibly* grand room. It did not belong underneath an Indian restaurant in the wild west section of an intergalactic theme park. It belonged in a palace, above ground, surrounded by luscious green gardens attended to by professional landscapers. It was a room fit for a king. As a matter of fact, in the corner of the room, there sat one.

'What brings you down here? Do you have news for me?'

The waiter nodded his head.

'Well then, what is it? Spit it out!'

The waiter took in a sharp breath.

'They've arrived, my grace, and I have overheard them talking about the contents of the floppy disk. They've mentioned our lord Gorgol by name. It looks to me like the plan has been executed without a hitch.'

'That is excellent news. Please let me know when they have finished their meals. I think it's about time I paid my daughter a visit.'

'Of course, King Guisher'.

The waiter turned and walked backwards through the door, so as not to turn his sweaty back on the king, and made his way back up the spiral staircase. He may have been about to deliver our heroes the mildest of curries, but things were definitely about to heat up.

*Kids Go Free\**

# XII

Gorgol sat in his ivory tower, formed from the transformed bones of the wilderwrawn. He was cold hearted, and had no remorse for what he had done over the many centuries that had passed since that day when he flew above the planet's surface, riding noble Deus, his pants full of faecal matter. Times had changed, and he now looked out over a sprawling sprawl of amusement park, the best rides seen for a hundred years. He also had a new pair of trousers that he'd woven himself. It had been a while since he had been out into the park and had a go on a ride, twenty-seven years actually, and he was amazed at the rapid change in fashion of rollercoasters. Every few years loop-de-loops would be popular and vertical drops would go out, log flumes would come and go, and those big seated drop things like the *Tower of Terror* at Disneyland would get taller and taller.

Why hadn't anybody bumped into Gorgol in all the years he'd been in the theme park? Well, his tower was in the rear of the park, and it housed a ride that no one had ridden on for a long time. *The Spooky Solicitor* was a walk through terror experience which robbed you of your sanity and wallet, whilst giving you the spookiest thrill of your life. Gorgol had ensured that he wouldn't get any unexpected visitors by unclipping and reclipping the rope which determined the direction of the queue for the ride, so that anyone wishing to gain their adrenaline rush from *the Spooky Solicitor* would end up in the *Mind Melder 3000*, having their mind melded and therefore not caring about the which ride they were on. Genius. And sometimes he would still manage to steal their wallets.

He could see something through the clouds that tingled his evil senses. He strolled up to the viewing platform, opened up his *Spooky Solicitor*-themed wallet, and pulled out a euro. He popped it in the slot and glanced through the binocular viewer. A space-limousine was touching down right where it should be and, if he squinted, he could just about make out the registration plate, R3V TR0Y.

'I had better send out a message to that pawn, King Guisher. It's time to crush any resistance, and destroy that blasted disk once and for all.'

Gorgol was a master of subtlety. He could pretty much get anything he wanted from people using his phenomenal good looks, his delicate charm and precise suggestion to warp and twist the minds of those he came into contact with. He wasn't afraid of silence, but he also never dominated a conversation when he needed to get his way. He held the ability to trigger the pleasure senses of other people by allowing them to talk about themselves, and he used phrases such as 'I can see your point but there's another perspective here'. Additionally he had a varied and dynamic intonation.

Monotone and repetitive patterns tend to diminish the

power of conversation and by keeping the conversation rich with variety, allowing the other person to talk but never settle on their own opinion, Gorgol was able to get whatever he wanted. He often walked into a room and within an average of seven minutes was receiving a foot rub from up to three people who all believed it was their own idea. In giving the aforementioned rub, they believed that their share price index would increase, libido return, and that their own feet would be rubbed similarly one day soon.

\*\*\*

It had been 50 years since Gorgol had met King Guisher and bent him to his will (prepare for a flashback). He had been riding wilderwrawn all day as the foundations of the theme park were being set. As he whipped the wilderwrawn with a whip made from his own back hair (yes, even truly beautiful aliens who have travelled the vortex have back hair), he heard a low rumbling noise that was unmistakably a ship landing on the planet. Gorgol was used to ships coming to the planet, pouring in the space-concrete that would one day soon house the most tremendous amusement park of the millenia, however the sound coming from the sky at this moment was different, it sounded more royal. Through the clouds burst an almighty ship shaped like a crown. It glided down and landed on the planet with a majestic bop.

'Here we go,' Gorgol said to himself, 'a king would be a powerful ally in the war to come. Let's go meet this ambassador of theme parks and monarch of the Tramalodrian System.' The wilderwrawn said nothing. Gorgol picked up his keys, wallet and water bottle (he was always hydrated, as he didn't care for the alternative) and travelled towards the crown shaped spaceship.

'Wow,' said King Guisher when he saw Gorgol, 'you really are something to behold aren't you? Utterly beautiful.'

'Yes,' replied Gorgol, varying his intonation, 'but tell me about yourself!'

'I am none other than King Gustavo Guisher III. I have come here to oversee the initial work on the most amazing theme park there ever will be, *Screaming Sam's Rickety Rocking Party Park*. In my humble opinion it's going rather well.'

'I can see your point,' said Gorgol, sneakily, 'but there's another perspective here...' Things were going great.

Within the space of about 30 minutes, Gorgol had King Gustavo Garibold Guisher III eating out the palm of his hand. There was no need for him to do this, but Gorgol just fancied seeing how far he could push the king, bending him to his will.

If you've ever eaten out of someone's hand you'll know

that it's not as pleasant as birds, horses and dogs make it look. In fact it is much more enjoyable to be the feeder than the person being fed, but King Guisher was not aware of this at the time.

That was how Gorgol had met the king, and after many many years had passed, King Guisher had become a very strong ally to have. He had access to weapons, armour and Sky TV. It was now that Gorgol was going to need to employ all of these assets in his bid to rid the world of that dastardly floppy disk and its ludicrous contents.

It was almost time for Gorgol to unite the spheres. He had known this day was coming. He had been told so a long time ago in his childhood, by his mother.

'One day the spheres will unite, Gorgol,' she had said over his bed while he was trying very hard to get to sleep. This was how he had known. His mother had been a very persistent individual. He hadn't slept at all that night.

Thanks to King Guisher's noble, monarchal esteem (and his two (!) credit cards) Gorgol had been able to amass a very large and destructive army beneath the earth (not Earth with a capital E of course, because this book is set in space!) over the next 50 years.

***

Back in the present, Gorgol knew that he had a bit of time. The travellers – his nemeses – would be hungry after their journey, and if they had any sense they'd be hitting *Chief Thunderous River's House of Spice*. Although they were his nemeses, and he knew he would be destroying them soon and reclaiming that all important artefact, the Disk o' Flop (floppy disk), he found himself hoping that they enjoyed their curry and got a vegetable biryani. During this time he decided to take the lift down to the Sub-sub-Basement of Dread and Despair to inspect his army (mainly for your benefit, so be grateful).

The lift door slid apart and Gorgol stepped out into the massive underground repurposed sports hall. In front of him thousands upon thousands of robotic soldiers, all designed to look like Gorgol's mother across the eight decades of her life stood to attention. Gorgol had some deep rooted parental issues but we won't go into them here, to avoid upsetting him. Some of the robots looked old and withered, like Gorgol's mother towards the end of her life, but they were still deadly. Others were much younger, slim and retro, wearing those yellow bikinis with pointy bra bits and had their hair beautifully curled.

Some of the robots were from Gorgol's mother's child rearing days and looked very tired and worn out. There was even a unit of pregnant mother robots whose bellies were set up to explode, launching a thousand grenades. Perhaps most extreme were the robotic variants of Gorgol's mother as a baby herself. Small, quick robots who cried out in a literally ear-piercing scream, who fired toxic acid from their vile mouths. This was quite the army, and would have been a diamond mine for Gorgol's psychiatrist.

Along the sidelines were tanks and catapults and all kinds of really cool futuristic war machines. The machinery was a breakthrough in electronics and engineering, even for space. The whole army was powered by reverse solar energy. This power had been invented by an unlikely engineer named Ribbling Dribbling who was a pretty piss poor electrician. He once accidentally switched two wires in a solar panel during the construction of the theme park and the rest was history. The robots fed on literal darkness. It gave them life, warmed their circuitry, and infused them with evility and hatred. This does not mean that they can be beaten by sunlight, or by flashing torches at them, don't be ridiculous. They could only be beaten the normal way, through violent force.

In the deep, deep, dark sports hall, the robots had been powering up for years, ready to burst forth and obliterate all they could on Gorgol's handsome command. With the spheres united and his nemeses now at the theme park in the same way a good Amazon order 'arrived as expected',

Gorgol knew it was time to release his horde into the park. He would make his master proud, in the hope that he would never walk a bowl of soup down those stairs again.

Gorgol went to a cupboard at the side of the sports hall and pulled out his flaming cloak. He put it on. He then reached out his perfectly formed hand, and lifted up a golden, diamond-encrusted microphone. He lifted the microphone to his mouth and gave the most awe inspiring speech there has ever been this side of the Drowecaps Nebula. It was amazing, full of words such as 'momentous', 'philiacorpenrensis', 'matriarchal' and 'mummy'. It has not been repeated here due to the fact that it would make you violently cry and laugh at exactly the same time, splitting your cerebral cortex right down the middle, killing you dead. The robots however were able to withstand the glorious speech, due to the fact they were robots. It really perked them up, getting them all riled and ready for a lovely big bloody battle.

Gorgol was ready, and with a monotonous, instructional voice, he spoke the activation code into the microphone, and then proceeded to drop the mic:

*'Mummy, please let me stay home, I've got chickenpox.'*

With this, the robot army began its march of destruction.

*with one full paying adult

# Chapter 13 (Unlucky for some)

The waiter reached the top of the staircase, paused, reached out his hand, and turned the thermostat up a few notches. The waiter's name was Ali, and he'd been working at this Indian restaurant for too many years. The number of bhajis that had passed by his fingers was outstanding.

Back at the table, a different waiter had been and gone with our heroes' meals. Biffin Bambright wiped some tikka masala from his ear. It was truly disgusting the way Mrs Bambright ate.

'Mr Carmichael,' he commented, 'that was a truly supreme meal. I can understand why you wanted to come back here after all of these years. I've never had a curry of this quality, and I spent my gap year in the Curryverse! It was the best. I would say though, next time I'll lay off the lime pickle, it was too much!'

But there was to be no next time. And you can never have too much lime pickle.

Stardew stood, as if to bring attention to herself, but then whispered so not to draw any glances from evil bystanders. She could really learn a lesson or two in public speaking from Gorgol.

'OK guys,' she started, both incon- and con- spicuously, 'we were on our way here to disseminate this floppy disk, then we decided it was too dangerous to do that because it looks like we've been tricked into coming here, but then we had to land because the parking had already been sorted and we had to pretend Mrs Bambright was the Reverend Troy McClusky to avoid suspicion right?'

'Right,' replied someone else at the table, it doesn't matter who.

'And then we had an incredible curry thanks to Mr Carmichael?'

'Yes, that literally just happened,' said Mr Carmichael.

'Enough of that sass. I'm just trying to figure out what we should do now. I think that as we're here, and we'd planned to come here all along, we may as well start giving out these floppy disks to people that can give it the attention it needs. Maybe head to the EU summit? They're probably really bored and could use a bit of excitement.'

'The EU *is* very boring,' replied an alien who looked just like Nigel Farage, who was sat at the table next to them and had started listening when Stardew inexplicably stood up.

It was now time for Phyllis to stand up. She was two inches smaller than Stardew but she was still dressed for a hen party and had massive (two inch) heels on. Therefore, she was about the same height as Stardew. Just an observation.

'I have something I need to tell you. I had been sworn to secrecy by the Police of Intergalactic Secret Services, the P.I.S.S.'

'Bloody space!' cried Mr Carmichael, spilling his mango lassi everywhere. 'You've been with them all along?!'

'Correct, Mr Carmichael. I also know what you did to your brother 20 years ago.'

'SPACE-FUCK!' he shouted, dropping Martin S. Ronson's lassi.

Phyllis looked over the team of heroes. They looked awesome.

'It is time to show the world what we've got, and disperse this sack of 10,003 floppy disks all over this god forsaken place. ARE YOU WITH ME?!'

'Yes,' said Martin S. Ronson, noticing how beautiful Phyllis looked when she was being bitchin'. Stardew piped up again.

'Phyllis – what the hell is going on here? Why did Troy McClusky set it up so we ended up on this planet?'

Phyllis sighed.

'I'm sorry I couldn't tell you before. I took an oath, and if I broke that oath I'd immediately wee myself, and then die. And then wee myself again. I was hoping my team could have made it here by now to take you all to a safe haven, give you back rubs and hand out those floppy disks to the EU diplomats officially, but I fear we've run out of time. Now it's too late, so I must officially make you reserve agents of P.I.S.S., then at least I can share my intel with you'.

An almighty roar echoed out around the theme park.

'What in the name of Space is that?!' exclaimed everyone at once, in an amazing coincidence.

Phyllis sighed.

'It's happening.'

'Hahaha!' Ali the waiter chuckled menacingly from the kitchen doorway, holding a shiny golden gun. 'Looks like dessert is off the menu!'

Phyllis swiftly took out a pistol from underneath one of her flaps and shot him in between the eyeballs, before he could even start making a joke about them not having time for a coffee.

'There's your tip, and keep the change,' she said, unable to decide on a single quippy one liner.

'OH MY GOD!' shouted Martin S. Ronson. 'You shot Ali the waiter!'

'He's in cahoots with the rest of them. Gorgol, the Reverend Troy McClusky, and... King Guisher.'

Stardew's face fell.

'What did you say?'

'That's right Stardew, your father, the king, is right here in this theme park.'

'Daddy? Here? Now? In this place? Here?'

'Yes,' replied Phyllis, 'and get used to it! He's a baddie,

and that's *no* mistake.'

Stardew took a deep breath, picked up her coat and shotgun and walked towards the door. The others followed. The camera panned around them in slow motion and you could see all the details of their incredible CGI alien bodies, especially Martin S. Ronson's which was having a slight reaction. Phyllis also looked fit, which Martin S. Ronson had noticed.

As they approached the doorway, Mr Carmichael whispered to Phyllis.

'Look, what happened twenty years ago…'

'It doesn't bother me Mr Carmichael. I know how it is, long nights on the road, not a soul to talk to, it eats away at you. It eats away and sometimes it is unleashed in the most horrendous ways. You are a good man. I know you are a good man.'

She opened the door.

'You're about to see something serious. Please brace yourselves.'

They all stepped outside. Mr Carmichael turned to Phyllis again.

'Thank you Phyllis. I will show you right here, right now, whatever is in store, that I *can* have my redemption, and I *CAN* do what is just and what is good!'

In an instant a beam of laser beam flew directly through

Mr Carmichael's pre-frontal cortex, sucking it inward, obliterating all that he was in mind and consequently in body, eliminating the memory of twenty years ago and destroying his whole life in a short instant. Death had come for Mr Carmichael and it had come straight from the barrel of Gorgol's space-sniper rifle.

He died.

'MR CARMICHAEL!' shouted Stardew, dropping to her knees, tears bursting out of her emotion tract. Memories came flooding into her mind. She remembered a particularly good cup of slime Mr Carmichael had brought her once, and running along the beaches on Diligord-4 with him behind carrying her bucket, spade and towel. She also remembered a time Mr Carmichael had got his tie stuck in a revolving door at the garden centre. Such good times they'd experienced together. His space-blood began oozing out of his skull, the greens and blues of his proteins, glucose, mineral ions and hormones he would no longer need due to the lack of life within his cells. A haunting moan began to echo from Stardew's mouth. She was devastated, knowing she would never experience another living moment with this metaphorical giant of a man ever again.

Mrs Bambright, Martin S. Ronson and Phyllis looked to where the shot had come from. Rising above the theme park was the most beautiful creature that they had ever seen. He was wearing a magnificent gown and flames surrounded him in a spectacle of annihilation. He lifted both of his perfectly formed alien arms at the same time.

'Today is the day of your reckoning,' said the creature, softly, but in the most commanding way possible. He really was a lovely looking thing.

'You are in possession of something, and I have come to take it.'

The wind was whirling, and from the angle that our heroes were standing they could see up the creature's skirt. They couldn't see everything, but they could see enough. Phyllis blushed and Martin S. Ronson got embarrassed.

'I am Gorgol, the Traveller, Bearer of Soup and Bringer of Destruction, Lord of the Wilderwrawn and Beauty of the Park of Themes. This is my army, and this is MY WAR!'

Biffin Bambright had had enough.

'Right! Hello, Mr Gorgol! Can you, or our new friend Phyllis, PLEASE enlighten me as to just what is going on here?! Why are we about to fight you?! Is it really all because of what's on that floppy disk?!'

Gorgol nodded.

'Very well,' Gorgol replied. 'It is only fair that a man about to embark into battle is aware of the reasons leading him there. The information on that floppy disk is merely a byproduct of a feud that has lasted millenia. You see, my master is the rightful monarch of this whole multiverse. When the spheres are aligned, they are at their peak power, and nothing, no one and no thing can oust them from their golden thrones.'

'Having seen what's on that floppy disk, I suppose that does make perfect sense,' replied Mrs Bambright.

'So are you ready then? Time to fight?'

'I guess so.'

Gorgol nodded again.

'I hope you enjoyed your biriyani, as it will be your last!'

'Actually, we all had tikka masala,' replied Biffin Bambright. For some reason, this angered Gorgol more than anything else in the last one thousand years.

'In that case,' he said with bits of anger dripping off him, 'you must welcome your imminent demise with open arms!'

He clicked his fingers and the ground began to rumble. Everyone fell over, except Martin S. Ronson who can't fall over. He looked around himself and his heart sank. Holes began to appear all over the theme park and hundreds of robotic Mothers of Gorgol began walking out, all kinds of sci-fi weaponry attached to their bodies.

Our heroes pegged it back inside the curry house. Martin S. Ronson decided to take charge.

'Okay, we need action, and action is what we need, and

we need that action now!'

Biffin Bambright replied.

'We need to get out of this curry house, via some kind of safe passage!'

A quiet voice whispered from behind them.

'I know – another way – out of this – curry house –'

It was Ali the waiter.

'I do not have much life left, because you shot me. The evil king had implanted a controlling device into my skull that forced me to do his bidding. You have done me a great service in destroying it, but a great disservice in killing me in the process. Swings and roundabouts I suppose.'

'WE DON'T HAVE TIME TO TALK ABOUT PLAYGROUND RIDES!' blurted out Mrs Bambright.

'I wasn't. It was a figure of speech. It means that the losses, setbacks, or negative aspects of a certain situation are cancelled out or balanced by equally advantageous or positive elements (or vice versa). Sometimes in life you are on a swing and sometimes you are on a roundabout, but sometimes a swing is good and a roundabout is bad (or vice versa).'

It was Stardew's time to interject.

'JUST TELL US WHAT YOU KNOW!'

'Yes, sorry, well, down in the basement there is an access hatch to a secret tunnel full of ammunition, armour, food, drinks and sweeties.'

'Great, let's go gang!' said Stardew excitedly.

'Hold on!' retorted Ali. 'It's a *secret* access hatch! The only way to enter it is through the secret unlock mechanism.' A smirk started to spread across Ali's face, looking at Stardew. 'I'll tell you the mechanism … for ten kisses.'

'Like *space* you will!' shouted Mrs Bambright, and shot Ali square in the head with a laser gun.

'Bloody Space!' shouted Stardew, 'why'd you do that?!'

'I'm not going to let him treat you like that, you should only kiss who you want to kiss, Stardew.' Bambright replied.

'No you idiot-brain, not kiss! K.I.S.S. stands for *Kurrency In Screaming Sam's*. It's the theme park-only currency that you can exchange for goods and services. Now we've got a dead waiter, knowledge of an access hatch, but no knowledge of how to open it.'

'Ah well, hindsight is twenty-twenty.'

'Oh for goodness sake, come on!'

Unbeknown to them, Ali had actually wanted to kiss Stardew 10 times, he had no need for K.I.S.Ses in the afterlife. Killing Ali had been the single most romantic thing Biffin Bambright had ever done, but now he was ashamed and embarrassed.

At that, they heard the familiar creak of an access hatch opening behind them. The two heroes rushed down the stairs, Stardew turning the thermostat back down on the way. They turned the corner to see Martin S. Ronson holding up a naan to a naan shaped hole in the wall and an open door next to him. Phyllis was looking very impressed and blushing slightly.

'Martin S. Ronson, how ever did you know that was how to open the access hatch?'

'Well...' started Martin S. Ronson.

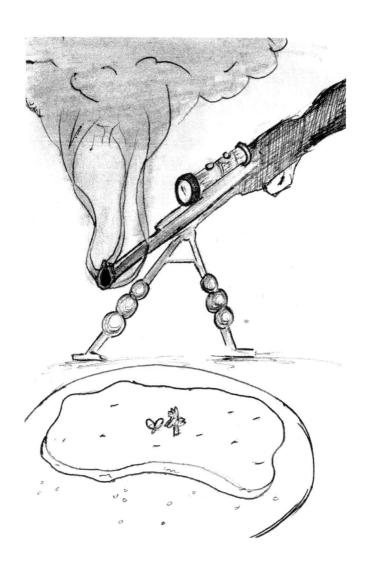

*A garlic naan, a smoking sniper and a lot of drama*

# Chapter 14:

# Triple Threat

Two hours later, Stardew (daughter of the king, in case you didn't know), Mrs Biffin Bambright, Martin S. Ronson and Phyllis, but not Mr Carmichael, were down the secret tunnel, loading up on all sorts of really cool sci-fi weaponry.

Stardew lifted up a deadly looking laser launcher which had metal spikes all around the edges and a gut-wrencher on the top.

'I'm going to call this *'The Carmichael'*.'

'That's a touching sentiment,' came a familiar voice from behind, which gave Stardew goosebumps. She turned. It wasn't Mr Carmichael, because he is dead. It was Martin S. Ronson.

'I hope you get to kick some epic battle ass with it.'

'Thanks,' replied Stardew.

The four of them had been sitting around discussing their best course of action.

'The problem is we need an army,' Stardew started. 'That Gorgol fella has thousands of those robots which look like variously-aged lady gargoyles for some reason. We've only got the four of us, and despite all these weapons and my excellent physique, I'm not sure we're good enough to take them on.'

The group sat and pondered for a while.

'Where are we going to get help? What we need is a large group of active, energetic, tall aliens to help us!' said

Martin S. Ronson.

'Basketball players!' Stardew ejaculated.

'Or how about some diplomatic, well meaning aliens that are reluctant to back down?' said Mrs Bambright.

'Diplomats!' Stardew exclaimed.

'Hmmm, we're also missing some pawns. Aliens with no future who will lay down their lives for us.'

'Poorly paid teenage rollercoaster attendants on zero-hour contracts!' Stardew exclaimed. 'RIGHT!'

'Let's split up. Go ahead and find those three comical groups of potential warriors and get them on our side. Meanwhile, I will think of an audacious way to disseminate these floppy disks to as many individuals as we possibly can. That's our main stake in all of this, and I'm worried it's been forgotten about because of all the cool other stuff that's happening.'

'Right you are captain!' said the other three all in unison in another one of those massive coincidences.

*The next three sections form the remainder of Chapter 14, and are presented to you side-by-side, in three columns, occuring at the same time, in parallel. Flip a three sided space-coin to decide which to read first! If you don't have a space-coin to hand, use a mirror!*

# Martin S. Ronson's Brave, Brilliant But *Bonkers* Basketball Bonanza

Martin S. Ronson shot off down the tunnel as fast as his little floating organ could carry him. In a short amount of time he found himself underneath the theme park's basketball court. He knew he was underneath the court for two reasons. The first was that he could hear the familiar sounds of basketball shoes

# Biffin Bambright's *Daring* Discovery of the Diplomats' Desires

Biffin Bambright had never been good at PE at school. His theory was spot on, but when it came to exerting himself physically he really struggled. This is why we now find him shooting down a tunnel on a golf cart, which is normally intended for staff use only, but the impending robot army and the high chance of

# Phyllis' *Technically* Tactful Transition of the Teenage Rollercoaster Attendants

The thing about Phyllis was that she was a business woman at heart. She used to live on the planet Yonem, a planet whose whole ecosystem revolved around money, as did its economy. She'd worked in stocks and shares. She'd been very good at the buy buy buy bit, and also very very good at the sell sell sell part.

squeaking and the ball bouncing up and down on the floor. The second was the sign that said 'Basketball Court Above'. He opened a small hatch above him, and burst straight out of the floor right into the middle of the final league game!

Now this match was really a sight to behold. There were very tall thin aliens, big blobby soggy aliens, and vaporous translucent aliens all zooming about in the most intense version of basketball that you've ever

death – made all the more real by Mr Carmichael's actual death – meant that rules needed to be broken.

Smashing right through a barrier, Mrs Bambright burst through the plaster wall of the *S.S.R.R.P.P.* Conference Centre (the *S.S.R.R.P.P.C.C.*), right into a room full of EU diplomats, tired of the conference and waiting for the part where they got to go on the theme park rides. As he hit the ground, he turned sharply to avoid

With her two skills working in tandem she had been very rich. However, after a few years in that job she'd reached the top, and that was when she'd transferred to being a top-secret spy for the Histapine Horticultural Husbandry corporation, as cover for her work with the P.I.S.S.

With that bit of backstory out the way, Phyllis popped on an inconspicuous mask and headed to the surface. It was a very busy day in the park, not only because of even thought about. Unluckily for our hero, he very quickly got mistaken for the ball. It was at this moment that Martin S. Ronson *disk*-overed something deep within himself that he had never known before – he was rather bouncy. While he was bouncing up and down and up and down, he was wondering to himself how he might be able to use this new *disk*-overy *[Editors note: please stop]* to his advantage in the coming war. He hitting an overhead projector, lifting the kart up on to two wheels with a huge screeching sound. It was now that Biffin Bambright wished he had attended all those jazzercise classes he had paid for, as his weight caused the kart to tip on top of him. He climbed out of his overturned kart, somewhat embarrassed, but glad that Stardew and the others weren't there to have seen it.

'Diplomats!' he roared. 'I have come here to give you a diplomatic choice! the robot army, the diplomat summit and the basketball tournament, but it was also the combination of half term, kids go free (with one full paying, four-limbed adult), and the standard 2-for-1 offer on the back of many cereal packets. For this reason, many poorly paid teenage rollercoaster attendants on zero-hour contracts had been offered lots of work.

Phyllis was by the *Shocker Rocker* log flume, the galaxy's only log flume to include never quite worked this out, but he did end up being the winning point for the Galactic Goofballs!

After he'd recovered, he launched himself at the commentator, knocking her out cold. He then grabbed the mic.

'Basketball players from across the universe! I need your help!' The two teams looked unimpressed.

'Outside right now is a tyrannical tyrant who is very determined to destroy our way of life. We need to Just outside here is a maniac with an army of robots designed to look like his mother. He is bent on the destruction of everything we hold dear.'

'So what?' shouted one diplomat with a tentacle for a nose, which is funny, even for aliens.

'We do not have to interfere unless we deem it necessary and logical for our respective planets. This one time while I was still an intern I interfered with a planetary system when it wasn't necessary or logical, real electric shocks.

She snuck up behind a sixteen-year-old chap named Chuffles. He was a nosnark, and his valves were pumping out noxious gases as normal. Fortunately, Phyllis' parents immunised her as a child, and the gases didn't turn her skin upside down like they were want to do. Amazingly, very poor health & safety training had left Chuffles in charge of the *Shocker Rocker* all on his own. Phyllis swiftly grabbed him round the neck, pulling rally together to stop him, and also there's this floppy disk that's really important too…'

Martin S. Ronson was starting to lose his confidence. The alien players were all giving him strange looks. You would probably think they all looked just like aliens usually look, but being an alien himself, Martin S. Ronson was able to understand subtleties of the alien expression, seeing doubt, annoyance and disappointment on

and I ended up twisting my ankle.' 'Ah yes,' added another, 'but we must all stand together in the name of diplomacy. I once went to a moon in the name of diplomacy and saved at least seven lunar species and it had no effect at all upon my ankle!' This alien had a normal nose, but also a nose where her tentacle should be.

Mrs Bambright looked around, thinking with haste. How could he convince these people of political

him down to the floor. Holding him there she whispered in his ears.

'Alright you, I need to get a message to the whole workforce, how do I do that?'

Chuffles was terrified, but being a sixteen year old, all he could focus on was Phyllis' gland which was pressing into his leg, which negated the terrification. Phyllis knew this and was slightly peeved that her gland was helping her in this way, but nevertheless, beggars can't be their faces/primary sensory limb. This was similar to the way that you think all sheep look the same, but actually they are looking at you with doubt, annoyance and disappointment, too.

'How do we know you're a good guy?' asked one of the basketball players, bouncing up and down on her long spring-shaped blue legs. Martin S. Ronson had been shot down. How would he ever convince these sportsaliens that he was a goodie, and not a baddie?

persuasion to fight for him? Then it came to him.

'A vote!' he shouted. The hall full of diplomats turned to each other and began chattering. A vote? They were used to diplomacy, *disk-ussions [Editors note: I'm done here]* and dealing with people in a sensitive and tactful way, but then again, they did love a vote. The chatter went on for a full minute, and all the while Mrs Bambright was thinking. Then it came to him.

'The sooner the

choosers.

'Erm, err, well all the staff carry pagers? You can page them all from the staff room over there.' He pointed toward the medium-sized brick building with a recognisable sloped roof, which clearly used to be a *Pizza Hut*.

'Thanks Chuffles,' said Phyllis, and she dropped him to the ground. Chuffles was in shock and he just sat on the floor watching Phyllis jog away. He vowed there and then that he would make her his wife. He never

'Ermm, well, you know the bad guys in *Space Jam*? If we lose, it will be like they won, and Bill Murray, Bugs Bunny and Michael Jordan were all for nothing!'

*Space Jam* was a very controversial film in sportsalien basketball circles, as although Michael Jordan was a hero of many alien basketball players, it was universally agreed that the film's portrayal of aliens was incredibly offensive. However, they got where Martin S. Ronson was coming

battle is over, the sooner you can all be let out to go on the rides!'

There was a roar of approval.

'Right, those who want to fight for the good guys and everything that is righteous and nice, stick your hand up.'

1,198 hands went up.

'And those who want to fight for the baddies, who will inevitably lose, put your hand up.'

1,106 hands went up.

Baffin Bambright whipped out his pocket calculator from somewhere.

did, but you should definitely remember him anyway.

Phyllis reached the staff room after doing some really cool rolls and flips in order to avoid the robot Gorgolmum scouts, which were starting to spread out around the park on patrol.

In the staff room she located the pager terminal. Luckily for her, and for us, it had no password and was very easy to use. She pressed 'send message to all staff' and wrote:

JOIN THE

from and despite her comment, the blue-legged alien player could easily tell he was a good guy just from looking at his little floating body and the way he had self-doubt but was struggling on anyway.

The two teams huddled together in an amazing show of sportsalienship that the league had never seen before.

'Okay, little orb. We're on your side. Let's do this for Bill Murray.'

'Okay. 1,198 plus 1,106 is 2,300 diplomats in total. 1,198 divided by 2300 equals 0.52. Multiplied by 100 this makes 52% for us goodies, which would mean, wow, 48% for the baddies. That's closer than I expected. Anyway. Everyone, TO WAR!'

RESISTANCE. DOUBLE PAY + PIZZA FOR ALL. MEET IN FRONT OF ROBOT ARMY IN 5 MINUTES.

She hit send. Phyllis looked out the window of the staff room over the park and was amazed to see hundreds, if not millions (it wasn't millions) of teenagers wearing *S.S.R.R.P.P.* uniforms, running towards the centre of the park.

'Wow, that was easy,' said Phyllis.

# Chapter

**01100110**
**01101001**
**01100110**
**01110100**
**01100101**
**01100101**
**01101110**

Now the army of the resistance was assembled, and oh what a mighty fine army it was. Basketball players, EU diplomats and teenage rollercoaster attendants had arranged themselves into a huge V shaped formation that sprawled out into the distance behind our four remaining heroes, who stood at the front of the V shape looking like absolute badasses. If/ when this is made into a feature film, that's probably the image that will be printed on promotional material, and at the end of the trailer. Perhaps it will even be edited so that they form the shape of a floppy disk. Incredible.

The massive V shape marched forward through the park, past *Smash Mouth's All Star Wild Ride*, past the Dodgems, right past *Chief Thunderous River's House of Spice*. Naturally, a massive V of people (aliens are people, too) doesn't always fit well inside the paths and tracks of a theme park, but they managed to sort of move about a bit and it was fine. Eventually the V shape stopped, squared up heroically to Gorgol and his motherly robot army. Stardew stepped forward in front of the rest of the characters.

'Gorgol! We are here to put an end to this!'

Gorgol laughed, quietly and matter of factly.

'My dear princess,' he retorted, 'you are fighting a losing battle. There is no way that you can defeat me – never mind my robot army – with this sorry team that you've assembled behind you.'

Stardew didn't know if she could beat Gorgol's great might and power. But she knew she had to try.

'Oh, I think you'll be *unpleasantly* surprised!' she screamed back, but with a whimper of uncertainty straining her voice.

'Listen, Princess! You know in your heart that this is a fool's errand. But I see potential in you, and your little band of friends. I didn't see any in the old man, which is why I shot him. Why not join my side? You can learn to serve and love the Master as I do. You can devote your life to the unity of the spheres. You can spread our message, and help what you saw on that floppy disk to become reality. You can join me. And you can join your father!'

Stardew took a step back. This would be a much easier option than fighting the seemingly unbeatable opponent and his hordes of deadly robot warriors. And it would be nice to see her dad again, even if she was miffed at him for stranding her on that terrible planet without its currencies and lines of credit. Additionally, this Gorgol guy was a lot more beautiful than she'd expected. He was positively bang tidy! But that was the wrong thing to do. And, ignoring that whole part where she blew up a planet because she'd overpaid for substandard yoffa, Stardew stood up for what was right.

'I'm afraid I can't do that.'

'Very well,' replied Gorgol. He raised his hand and fired out a thin, white beam from his palm, that hit Stardew directly in the chest.

'Noooooo!' shouted Martin S. Ronson.

A massive white flash momentarily blinded everyone. When their sight returned, Stardew was gone.

'You heartless, cruel villain!' screamed Martin S. Ronson. 'Prepare for WAR!'

This was not a great thing to say, as Gorgol had been preparing for this war for over 900 years, so was pretty well versed in the act. It sounded epic though.

\*\*\*

You might have thought, reasonably, that Stardew was dead at this point in our story. Our heroes did. Everyone in the V shape formation did. But Gorgol knew otherwise.

Stardew, who had braced herself for impact, lowered her hands from her face and opened her eyes. She wasn't where she had been standing seconds previously. She didn't know where she was. She was in a small, glass cell, floating in a seemingly endless void.

'What the...?'

She tried to bash on the side of the glass. It behaved strangely, unlike any glass she had bashed before. When she struck it, the glass rippled away from the point of impact, all the way around the cell until the waves interfered with each other and fizzled out.

'Seriously. What the hell.'

She sat back down in the middle of the cell, out of ideas.

'Stardew…'

A voice echoed out, seemingly coming from everywhere at once. She knew that voice.

'Look who's decided to show up!' she screamed out into the abyss. 'Years! Years you left me on that *awful* Diligord-4 or -5 or whatever it was with no way of contacting you. And now you don't even have the stones to show your face!'

The cell jerked outwards, until it was about four times the size it had been previously, and King Guisher popped into existence in its centre. Stardew stood up.

'Where the hell have you been?' she asked him.

'Everywhere, nowhere. Mainly in a cage much like this, waiting for my time to serve Gorgol. And now that time has come.'

'Why the hell are you helping that vile beast?!'

'Have you not seen his beauty?'

'You can't get on board with a tyrant just because he's beautiful, I've already had that brief but poignant realisation.'

'Well, yes. It was his beauty at first, but then he began to talk. He talks with such conviction, such grace. If you just gave him a chance and a foot rub, Stardew…'

'I will not be corrupted by him.'

'Please, daughter. Join me, we can bring peace to the universe and you can marry Gorgol and eat soup for the rest of your days.'

'Join you?! After you left me on that ghastly planet for all those years? Soup?'

'My dearest...' and at this point the King uttered Stardew's real name, which dedicated readers (the kind we like) will remember is not only so difficult to pronounce that your speech systems are required to vomit three times in order to get the correct timbre on the first syllable, but it also cannot be typed with a QWERTY keyboard. At hearing her real name Stardew shuddered and shivered at the same time. The King continued, '… I only took you to Diligord-4 and signed you up to that boring governing role to keep you safe from the destruction that was all around us. Look at you now, so strong and independent, so knowledgeable and wise. With you on my side we can be a family again.'

King Guisher reached out his gloved hand, all eight fingers stretching to clutch the hand of his only (legitimate) daughter. Despite all his evil, at this one moment, he truly wanted his daughter back.

A single space-tear rolled down Stardew's pointed

cheek, but she kept her own hands, ungloved, where they were.

'I'm sorry father, I cannot join sides with someone so evil. I just can't stoop that low.'

King Guisher's gaze turned, and an evil smile appeared at the corners of his fleshly, kingly lips.

'In that case, daughter, I have no option but to end you.'

'I'd like to see you try.'

The king pulled two equally matched sci-fi swords from straight out of the cage floor and threw one to Stardew.

'This can't be an execution. There's no glory in an execution. I shall defend Gorgol's glory through battle, and I shall make him proud!'

He lunged at Stardew, but she did a badass backflip and avoided his blade. The glass cage grew massively in size and a bunch of cool platforms appeared to allow a climactic sword fighting scene to take place unhindered.

\*\*\*

Martin S. Ronson's days of pacifism were over. As far as he was aware, Gorgol had not only killed Mr Carmichael, but now Stardew too, and he was also about to attempt to unite the spheres and cause untold misery and administrative tasks across the Universe, as well as most likely killing him and a few others in the process. This had made him absolutely *livid*.

'Prepare for WAR!' he had recently said, just before the Stardew bit.

'Oh, little orb, I have spent the last one thousand years preparing for this war (he had slightly exaggerated). Do you really think that you can defeat me with this motley crew that you've managed to rustle together?'

'Oh yes. Yes I do.'

'You are a fool. Have you forgotten that your presence here is all a part of my plan?!'

Martin S. Ronson was a little bit sick in his mouth. He'd got all excited by the way the story was going and actually had forgotten that part. Martin S. Ronson reluctantly swallowed the sick back down to save face. It didn't work. Gorgol continued.

'I can see from the little bit of sick in your mouth that yes, you have forgotten that this was all part of my plan!'

'Why are we here?!' shouted Martin S. Ronson. 'Please, tell me what's brought us here?!'

Gorgol laughed.

'Now that it's too late for you to turn back, I will fill you in. You see, I need to unite the spheres. The thing is, I couldn't complete that task without the final piece of the puzzle. You know how to unite the spheres, don't you?'

'Of course!' replied Martin S. Ronson. 'It's on the intergalactic Key Stage 3 curriculum! But it's not possible! They only teach us so we can look out for signs that somebody is planning on uniting them so we could tell an adult!' He gesticulated towards Gorgol. '*Somebody's* classmates obviously weren't paying attention!'

'Why do you say it's not possible, little one?'

'Whoever is to unite the spheres needs to possess the three tenets of sphericity – the head of an oxelquarf, which has been extinct for millions of years, the hooves of a moroquench, who evolved hands back in the bronze space-age, and the heart of a princess, which can be stolen either literally or figuratively!'

Gorgol pulled out a brown, threadbare cloth from his left pouch. He unravelled it and the contents made Martin S. Ronson even sicker in his mouth. Shrouded in the blanket were two things Martin S. Ronson had never expected to see.

'Oh my illuminated manuscript. It's the head of an oxelquarf. The hooves of a moroquench. You have two of the three tenets of sphericity! Why did you evaporate Stardew when you could have taken her heart?!'

'Oh, floaty boy, I didn't evaporate the princess. I merely sent her to an ephereal cage in the void! In fact, right now, either her father has turned her to my side so I can steal her heart figuratively with my good looks and charm, or he's about to split her chest cavity open in a badass sword fight!'

\*\*\*

Stardew did a double-backflip off a really high platform onto a lower platform, that was still really high, and moving at speed horizontally. As she landed, the platform crumbled, and she fell through the air towards the floor of the cage. In an attempt to not die, she plunged her sword into the side of the cage, and the friction slowed her down enough that by the time she reached the floor, she was moving at a low enough velocity that she didn't even hurt her feet. This sword fight was gearing up to be totally extravagant.

The king did exactly the same thing at exactly the same time, but in a mirror image on the other side of the cage, which made the whole thing even more badass. As they simultaneously landed, a shockwave echoed across the glass cave which caused it to contract in on itself, so it was only a few feet wide again. Both characters thrust their swords towards each other but managed to twist their bodies in such a way that they both avoided impact, and the swords ended up in the side of the cage.

This then made the cage expand out to be massive again, but the king and his daughter had effectively swapped sides because their swords were stuck into the opposite side that they had thrust from. Honestly, if this was a film it would look so, so cool, but it's not, so just imagine it.

They each yanked their sword out of the side of the cage, which caused two, huge holes to appear in both places. They both hit the floor. A massive force from the void began to pull on each of them through the holes, and it took all of their might to remain with their feet planted on the floor.

Eventually, the strain was too much for the king to bear, and he stabbed his sword straight down into the bottom of the cube. This allowed him to regain his balance, but caused the holes to rip apart across the whole fours side of the cage. The top part of the cage then fell down onto the bottom part, which meant that the pulling force could no longer affect the two fighting relatives, but also meant that the cube was running on really shaky foundations.

At this point the glass cage was under so much stress that the roof started to disintegrate, which meant it started to *rain shards of glass*. I *know*! Stardew ran across the cage towards her father, dancing in and out of the shards of glass, while he put up a hood that was made of metal chains which meant he was way more protected against the falling glass.

What he wasn't protected against was Stardew's swordsalienship. She lurched at him, and with a sweeping, crescent-shaped motion, she sliced through his sword weilding arm.

'Ahhhh!' he screamed out in pain. His hand didn't drop the sword, but he did lose the arm it was attached to, which had pretty much the same effect.

Although he had been disarmed, he wasn't ready to give up the fight. As Stardew came in with a second blow, he ducked underneath her and did a three hundred and sixty degree spin, taking her sword with his other hand as he went. He stood up as she turned around, and they locked eyes.

Stardew was about to say a really clever line about his arm being chopped off, but before she could say anything a huge shard of glass zoomed past, just in front of her face. She was lucky that it didn't fall on her head, which would have killed her, but was unlucky too, because it had sliced her nose clean off.

She was bleeding quite a lot, as was her father, the king, because when you lose an arm quite a lot of blood comes out. Same with the nose. They both started to feel intensely light-headed.

King Guisher knew that he had to return to Gorgol with his daughter's heart, otherwise he wouldn't be able to unite the spheres. If he died before transporting her back, she would be left to rot in the glass cage, as she had no idea how to transport herself out, and he hadn't told Gorgol where in the void he'd placed the teleportation receiver. He accepted now that this was a massive oversight. If his daughter died in the void without her heart being in the possession of Gorgol, the spheres would never be reunited (unless they could find another princess, but most of the universe was a republic now, so there weren't many of them left).

Stardew had collapsed in the centre of the cage, with shards of glass raining down on her, each piercing blow bringing her closer and closer to death. The king tried to raise his sword so that he could finish Stardew and take her heart, but he'd lost too much blood to have the strength to get the sword above his waist. He felt himself collapsing too. In his final act of consciousness, he pulled the transportation ray out of his satchel, and shot them both.

\*\*\*

The horgonian chef was sitting in the curry house staff room having a cigarette break. She was smoking three cigarettes at once, one in each of her primary nostrils, none in her secondary. You may be aware that horgonians are one of the few races that actually receive huge health benefits from smoking and her health was tip top. She was completely unaware of anything that was going on, she'd never even heard of Gorgol, let alone been in cahoots with him. She was literally just the chef.

It was because of this that she was incredibly startled when the king and his daughter appeared instantly in the underground room at *Chief Thunderous River's House of Spice*, both bleeding. They were unconscious.

'Oh my GOD!' she screamed, in some alien language. 'I'd better find a security guard!'

She hopped out of the room in the classic horgonian style. She never found a security guard – she actually went straight to her car and drove home.

Stardew slowly opened one eye. She guessed she was back in the curry house. Her eye backed up this fact. She opened her other eye, and her third (whether this eye was real or figurative, we do not know). She turned her eyes and head round to see her father on the floor next to her, all bruised and battered. She knew he'd wake up soon, the aroma from the saag aloo was too pungent to maintain slumber.

Adrenaline is an amazing thing. Also known as epinephrine, it has the incredible ability to make injured, tired and worn out characters able to resume full recovery after falling down big holes, getting shot in the shoulder, being punched a lot or having their arm/nose sliced off.

With this vital piece of knowledge in mind, Stardew grabbed her sword from out of her father's hands and ran straight out the door (she didn't weave, zig-zag or anything, just bombed it straight outta there).

Out of the door she witnessed a colossal scene. The sky was a deep red, and there were explosions all about the horizon. She could see a host of basketball players storming out of the tropical jungle part of the park, led by Martin S. Ronson who was riding an awesome thunder steed with a four-pronged trident in his hand. Coming towards the golplorx was Biffin Bambright, who looked stunning in a purple leotard clasping a flamethrower in one hand and swinging a flail in the other. He was ripping into mother-robots all around him, which were falling to the ground in a flaming heap. Around him were many, many, diplomats, all of whom had various types of blaster in their hands and were equally dispensing of robots, while shouting '*Diplomatise this!*'. Stardew heard a rumble from behind. She turned to see Phyllis riding in a log flume cart, followed by hundreds of young *S.S.R.R.P.P.* workers, all in various-sized roller coaster carts. Some were small, single seaters in which the drivers were holding spears from the hook-a-duck game, others were much larger, with three or four riders, acting more like tanks with air rifles and laser pistols.

The battle was in full flow.

*The crossed swords of an estranged father-daughter*
*relationship*

# Chapter the Sixteenth

Biffin Bambright was not in a good place mentally. All he was thinking to himself was '*SHIT! Shit, shit, shit.*' What the hell was he doing wearing a purple leotard?

He was also regretting his choice to wield both a flamethrower and a flail at once. The flail, which is effectively a spikey ball on a chain, was spinning so fast he wasn't sure he could stop it, and he feared for his life, more from his own hand than the robots who were daring enough to come near him. If that weapon so much as touched him, he'd be reduced to a wet steaming pile of chicken liver, instantly. It wasn't your average medieval flail, like the ones you're used to, no! It was a *Space-Flail 4003*. At the centre of the weapon was a very small unstable star, and the spikes were made of pure anthrax. You really didn't want to get touched by this bad-boy. How it even existed was a mystery that not even Mr Carmichael (space-rest his soul) could have solved and as for where it came from, well, good question.

The flamethrower on the other hand (quite literally) was pretty standard, pouring out flame like it was a liquid from the tap of hot death. Mrs Bambright looked around, his bottom lip quivering as he sprinted through wave after wave of robots. He suddenly halted, the flail still spinning of course, and he found himself face to face with none other than his good friend Martin S. Ronson.

Our original hero, whom we have all come to know

and love, was right in the throws of war. The small floating orb's heart was pounding with a tempo of power, wisdom and courage, in the time signature 3/8. He had focus and poise as he rode his elegant beast which he felt at one with, like their very souls were connected and were at a point of convergence, a singularity of desire and destiny.

He swung his four-pronged blue-crystal trident around him, sending streams of robots flying in all directions, which exploded upon impact. He then slammed the bottom of the trident into the ground and turned to look at Mrs Bambright. The shock from the trident echoed across the ground like a ripple in a lake, and as the ripple shot out, robots fell to the ground, nuts and bolts clattering, making the audience go *woah* in amazement. He was the embodiment of a true leader to his group of basketball players, and they were running alongside him (unmounted as they already had long legs/tentacles/fronds/wheels).

One of the basketball players was carrying a banner with the late Mr Carmichael's face on it, becoming the symbol of the resistance. Where she'd managed to get this banner was a mystery that was never solved, as she also died during the battle and the banner was taken by a diplomat to carry, and subsequently forgotten about.

'How's it going Martin S. Ronson?' said Biffin, panting and hoping that his war-colleague was also a bit shaken by this whole experience.

'My dear Bambright!' the golplorx said, 'I am in my element! I fight for virtue and justice and all that is floppy and obsolete! We will bring the dark lord Gorgol to his knees and make him wish he'd never entered this dimension! Praise the sun!'

'Err, yeah... me too, I've killed lots of robots!' Biffin continued, the flail spinning, and spinning, and spinning, 'and possibly a few teenage casual staff who got in the way!'

'Come my friend, mount my steed and let us ride together with this band of courageous basketball players and diplomats! Phyllis is flanking the left side with her team of merry workers, we must flank the right!'

Martin S. Ronson reached out his hand to grab Biffin Bambright by the leotard, and he hauled him up onto his horse. However, due to Mrs Bambright's accelerated heart rate and flustered demeanor, he let go of his space-flail in his attempt to mount the beast.

The speed of the spinning weapon had been tremendous, and Biffin's release caused it to fly high into the air with a fantastic *whoosh* noise. Both of our heroes followed the flail with their eyes as it flew in a beautiful curve, stardust trailing away behind it. Gravity did its trick and began pulling it towards the ground.

*FFFFIIIIUUUUUPP!* went the ball as it collided with

the centre of the Festival Square, the crux of the theme park and the place where most parents tell their children to head towards should they get lost. The impact caused the huge density of atoms in the unstable star to begin expanding. A few children were lost (as in killed, not just seperated from their parents) in the impact. The star grew larger and larger, ripping apart the tarmac covered ground of the Festival Square. It grew and grew, eventually becoming a golden sphere with a radius of about 30 metres. At its full size, cracks began to show on the ball and light burst forth from its centre. A shattering sound filled the square and the sphere suddenly fell in on itself into a crescendoing singularity. A black hole formed in the crater, and everyone on the planet, as well as every inanimate object, felt a gentle tug pulling them towards it.

Had the *Space-Flail 4003* slipped from Mrs Bambright's fingers just a split instant later, it would have gone straight into the ground and the black hole would have sucked both Biffin and Martin S. Ronson into it, causing the rest of the story to result in disaster, and Gorgol to unite the spheres and rule in tyranny forever more. Just think about that for a moment – that is the sheer danger that our characters are in.

'Oh holy space tits,' said Mrs Bambright in a very downhearted kind of way, 'this whole thing is bloody ridiculous.' He glanced up to Martin S. Ronson and expected to see a look of disappointment. Instead, however, Martin S. Ronson was looking quizzically at the black hole which was slowly pulling in a falafel stand and the body of a balloon salesalien dressed as a squid, as well as all her balloons, even though they were helium ones. As these objects fell into the hole they became stretched over a long distance, giving the impression of them falling away eternally. There was then a small pop, and the object disappeared.

'Biffin, do you have the instructions for that there space-flail?' said Martin S. Ronson, in full peak of his character arc, and as cool as a cucumber. He knew it was specifically a *Space-Flail 4003,* but he was saving time.

'Of course I do, the number one rule at *Biffin Bambright's Bodacious Body Shop* was *always keep the instructions.'* He reached his large hands deep down into the purple leotard and ruffled around. Martin S. Ronson averted his eyes and glanced back at the destruction all around him. How had his life come to this? Around them were the bloody, mutilated and lifeless bodies of three groups of people who should never have come to this: basketball players with their unique but individually special body shapes and skills, diplomats, their minds always focused on managing international/planetary/galactic relations, and many, many teenage rollercoaster attendants, who didn't stand a chance, and were somewhat lied to in an attempt to get them to lay down their lives for some aliens they'd never met and a floppy disk.

The floppy disks! Martin S. Ronson had almost forgotten about them! He had a huge space-sack full of thousands and thousands of copied floppy disks, and he needed to get them out to as many people as possible before the evil Gorgol destroyed them all.

Biffin triumphantly pulled out the instructions, and using his excellent skills as a mechanic and generally useful person, he flicked to the *Side Effects* section.

'Says here: *should your Space-Flail hit the ground at a terrific speed, it may fall in on itself and form a black hole. Be warned, this black hole can act as an intergalactic wormhole, sending any objects that fall into the hole to random inhabited planets elsewhere in the universe. Do not stick your fingers in!'*

'So what you're saying,' Martin S. Ronson said, 'is that anything we throw into that hole is immediately teleported through a wormhole to another planet somewhere else in the universe?' He now had a slight smirk on his face.

'Well yeah, I guess so, and the planets will always be inhabited, I suppose that's just a fact of how black holes work, something to do with the relationship between consciousness and dark matter that was discovered in the twenty-third century,' replied Mrs Bambright. 'Why are you smirking?'

'Don't you see, Biffin? We can use this to our advantage! All we need to do is pour all these thousands of floppy disks into that there hole, and they will be sent out across the universe, uniting people with the truth and beauty that is within their 1.44 MB memory!'

'Wow, that is quite a plan!'

Despite the excellent plan, Biffin looked solemn for a moment, staring away over Martin S. Ronson's metaphorical shoulder.

'Hey, Martin S. Ronson?'

'Yes, Mrs Bambright?'

'We've come quite a way in this madness of a story. Thinking back to the day a dirty ol' golplorx floated into my shop, I never thought it would end up like this.'

'Woah, please. I'm not dirty, or ol'.'

'Sorry, sorry! Just a force of habit,' replied the alien who was now even more solemn. 'I guess what I'm trying to say is that no one could have guessed what would have become of our lives after our first meeting.'

'My friend, I know exactly what you're trying to say. This whole adventure has been totally crazy and haphazard. We've taken so many unpredictable twists and turns. Five stars. All we can do is run with what's happening, and remember that when this is all over, it was quite the ride.'

This wasn't what Biffin Bambright had been trying to say, but before he could find the words to say what he had been trying to say, Phyllis' log-flume cart came screeching to a halt alongside the pair.

'Hey guys! I've just seen Stardew emerge from a doorway over there, she looks in pretty bad shape. She's got no nose! I think it's time we regrouped and brought this son of a bitch Gorgol to justice!'

Phyllis looked longingly at Martin S. Ronson as he gave his horse a gentle kick to get him going. Biffin jumped into the cart alongside Phyllis. He turned to Martin S. Ronson.

'Hey little buddy, if it's alright with you, can we tell Stardew that I'd planned to cause a black hole to disseminate the floppy disks across the universe on purpose?'

The small floating orb turned to Biffin Bambright, his best and only space-bro, and gave him the smallest of nods.

'Did you hear me, Martin S. Ronson?'

'Oh sorry, yes I did,' he replied, realising he should have given a bigger and better nod.

\*\*\*

Meanwhile, Stardew had witnessed the whole thing as she gallantly fought her way through the battle towards her friends. She never did tell Mrs Bambright that she'd seen him accidently let go of his flail, and the look of sheer panic on his face as it hit the ground. Stardew was very kind that way.

Martin S. Ronson, Phyllis and Biffin Bambright came hurtling towards Stardew.

Martin S. Ronson shouted towards her.

'Hey! Stardew! Biffin's set a great plan in motion! We're going to fling all the floppy disks into the black hole, sending them all over the universe!'

'Wow, great plan Mrs Bambright! Let's do this shit!'

Suddenly a voice sounded from behind the group.

'NOT SO FAST! WE HAVE UNFINISHED BUSINESS TO ATTEND TO!'

It was the king! He had woken up, and was coming back for Stardew.

'It's my father, he's woken up and is coming back for me,' said the only character for whom it made sense to say that line. Which was Stardew. If you didn't get that, then you're a lost cause. 'Right. Biffin, come with me, Phyllis and Martin S. Ronson, you get those disks in to that hole!'

'But what about Gorgol?' asked Phyllis. 'He's still leading the army!'

'I think we've got to face the sci-facts here,' Stardew replied. 'His army outnumbers ours massively. The future of the universe as we know it relies on those floppy disks.

Getting them into that black hole is the most important thing in the world at the moment.'

'In the world?' piped up Martin S. Ronson. 'Don't you mean in the universe?'

'Precisely. Let's do this.'

Martin S. Ronson jumped into Phyllis' log flume cart, and they shot off down the hill. Stardew grabbed Biffin's hand in a heroic platonic kind of way, and they ran off towards the king, who was standing in the doorway, awaiting his destiny.

Stardew and Biffin approached the king.

'Well what have we got here then?' he said, slightly woozy from the lack of blood, but still focused enough due to that adrenaline thing we mentioned earlier. 'Looks like a couple of prim plums, prime for the picking.'

You can tell that he was still woozy because of that weird insult.

'What are you on about?' said Biffin.

'You've lost, father! You only have one arm and don't have a sword. Give up. Come with us quietly. I'll get you into hospital and we'll sign you up for *evil-be-gone* classes. In 6 to 9 months we can be like father and daughter again, just like mum would have wanted.'

'Don't you dare say her name!' retorted King Guisher.

'I didn't! I just said –'

'ENOUGH! This ends here and now. We need your heart, but Gorgol didn't say anything about your friend with the cylindrical head!'

He reached behind his back, then pulled out a space-gun. In a matter of quickness, he lifted the weapon and shot at Biffin Bambright.

Stardew threw the sword *ridiculously quickly* to Biffin, who, being super quick himself (and suddenly incredible at combat) managed to bounce the laser off the sword and into the sky. More lasers came from the gun and he continued to bounce them all off the sword. *Szoo, szoo, szoo,* went the lasers before a *ping, ping, ping,* as they bounced off the sword.

'You can't keep this up for ever!' said the king.

'Well yeah,' replied Biffin, through gritted teeth. The *szoo szoo szoos* and the *ping ping pings* kept on going.

Biffin was concentrating so flipping hard on the task at hand, which as I'm sure you're thinking was a nearly impossible task as it is.

Suddenly, something flew from the side and hit the king's gun, jolting it to the left. A laser shot forth from the barrel of the gun. It smashed into a nearby frog-shaped bin at the perfect angle, bouncing straight back, but just slightly higher, and straight through the forehead of King Guisher III.

Biffin picked up a floppy disk from the floor, and simply said:

'It looks like it really was curiosity that killed the cat.' He instantly regretted saying it. He turned to look at Stardew who had thrown the disk in the first place.

She fell to her knees and stared straight at the lifeless body of her king, and more importantly, her father. Her expression was giving nothing away at all. She just stared. Biffin dropped the sword and edged closer to his friend, bending over to look at her to see if anything would show how she was feeling. He had no idea.

After about two minutes, which felt, not like a lifetime because that's just stupid, a bit longer than two minutes, say five, Stardew stood up. She turned to Mrs Bambright and gave him the biggest smooch on his big fat alien lips that you could think of. Absolutely disgusting. Biffin didn't feel so self-concious in his purple leotard now.

***

From the cart, Phyllis and Martin S. Ronson spied a group of diplomats, who were pushing a huge ballista (a catapult used in ancient warfare for hurling large stones) up the hill. They had been firing makeshift bombs made from the prizes at the amusements. Large explosive Spongebobs and Patricks. The bombs were having no effect. Something more drastic needed to happen.

'Get me in there, Phyllis, and fling me over the black hole!' came a voice that we, and you, didn't expect to hear again.

Phyllis and Martin S. Ronson looked around the cart. It was Chuffles, the teenage rollercoaster attendant, who had exclaimed that previous line. Remember him? Good. He'd been following Phyllis ever since her technically tactful transition of the teenage rollercoaster attendants, and he'd fallen in love with her. Bet you didn't expect to see Chuffles again did you?

Chuffles was Chuffles' last name, but everybody called him by it, as if it were his first. He was raised by Mr and Mrs Chuffles in a small, suburban commuter town about thirty miles from the planet's capital city.

Chuffles had a lot to live for – this rollercoaster attending job was just something he did on the weekends while he was saving up to attend university. He'd already been accepted to study Mechanical Engineering at one of the Tralmordian System's finest universities, and a long, glistening career with private health insurance and performance based bonuses was sure to follow (unbeknown to Chuffles however, every sixteen year old in the Tralmordian System wanted to be a mechanical engineer so they could build rollercoasters, and the industry was saturated). Why then was Chuffles so eager to be flung over the black hole, which is so obviously a recipe for catastrophe?

Well reader, Chuffles had fallen deeply in love with Phyllis. Her suckers made him weak at the knees. The blue tinge of WKD on her lips reminded him of sweet, sweet summers spent as a child frolicking through woodland without a care in the world. He wanted to show Phyllis what he could do, and win her heart.

Phyllis was definitely not interested. In fact, she hadn't even noticed Chuffles' infatuation with her.

'OK! I guess that might help!' she shouted, and with great strength (and a little doubt) she turned the big wheel of the ballista, increasing the tension in the mechanism. Chuffles struggled to climb up into the bowl. His trousers were slipping down a bit, he'd forgotten his belt today just like his mother always said he would. With his cheeks going green (the same way your cheeks go red when you're flushed), he rolled onto his back into the bowl, like a rotund person trying to get into a boat.

'Okay Chuffles, are you ready?' said Phyllis.

'Erm, I think so,' said Chuffles, lying on his back, his many chins (just a feature of his alien body) wiggling all over the place, 'except maybe this wasn't such a good idea...'

Phyllis released the handle. Chuffles was launched way over the black hole in the direction of Gorgol.

'I WON'T LET YOU DOWN PHYLLIS!' Chuffles shouted. 'I LOV–'

He was pulled straight into the black hole with a gentle pop. Gone. The gravity in those things really is immense.

'Balls!' shouted Phyllis. She knew it was 50/50 that the poor attendant would be sucked through the wormhole, but had hoped he would have made it to Gorgol to at least buy her a few seconds to think through her plan. She turned to Martin S. Ronson.

'What do we do, Martin S. Ronson?! What do we do now?!'

'I don't know, but we need to stop him!'

Martin S. Ronson had noticed Chuffles' lust for Phyllis, he'd been a teenager himself. He was slightly pleased that Chuffles was no longer a romantic rival for Phyllis' heart, but did feel pretty bad for even thinking this.

He pointed at Gorgol, standing atop *Smash Mouth's All Star Wild Ride*, who had watched the demise of King Guisher, and had now resigned himself to the fact that he was going to have to get his own hands dirty if he was going to steal the princess' heart and get those darned spheres united. Gorgol sighed and lifted both his hands (palms up) at once, which also lifted him into the air. Turning his palms forward, Gorgol floated in that direction, then he bent his hands down slightly and floated towards the ground. All the while, his cloak of one-hundred apocoli (space-plural of apocalypse) was flaming. Reaching the surface, he stood about a metre and a half away from Stardew, daughter of the ex-king, and Mrs Bambright of *Biffin Bambright's Bodacious ex-Bodyshop*.

'Nice outfit,' he said to Biffin. 'Where'd you get that from, Aldi?!'

Stardew giggled. Yes, Gorgol was mean and about to destroy the whole universe, but he was *so handsome.*

'Oh no!' Martin S. Ronson shouted from afar. 'He's stealing her heart!'

Biffin retorted.

'It *is* from Aldi, actually! Space-Aldi! The clothes are just as good quality as those in Space-Sainsbury's, but they're half the price!'

'Oh my god, that's so lame!' said Stardew, turning towards Gorgol and smiling with her eyes and lips.

'Yeah,' replied Gorgol, 'that's so super space-lame. I can't believe you got your clothes from Space-Aldi. I wouldn't be caught *dead* in an outfit from Space-Aldi. In fact, I'd rather *be* dead...'

A huge explosion erupted from where Gorgol was standing. The sound was deafening. Dust filled the air.

Everybody stopped what they were doing.

The dust settled.

Stardew gasped.

Biffin Bambright wiped a tear away from his eye. His feelings were really hurt at the whole Space-Aldi thing. He then started paying attention again and also gasped.

Where Gorgol had just stood, what used to be Chuffles was lying in a decimated heap. He had fallen through the black hole, but in a massive coincidence he had ended up being fired out of a wormhole at an incredible velocity, about 10,000 kilometres above where Gorgol was just stood. Travelling at this speed killed him instantly, but his body continued to move through space until it reached Gorgol, where it smashed into him with the power of one billion bendy buses.

This was too much for even Gorgol to withstand.

Intertwined with Chuffles was the lifeless body of Gorgol in his true, disgusting form, the form he had been born with, the form with which he had served the Master soup for millennia. Everyone was disgusted. Disgusting. Stardew threw up.

'Can we get rid of him?' she asked. She was really embarrassed that she had just been flirting with this creature. She *should* have been embarrassed that she had been flirting with a creature who was so horrible on the *inside* anyway, but I guess that's the universe we live in.

'My pleasure!' exclaimed Mrs Bambright. He picked up the entangled bodies of Chuffles and Gorgol, and launched them into the black hole.

'Quickly, get these in there too! We can finally finish this crazy adventure!' shouted Martin S. Ronson, pointing at the floppy disks. Mrs Bambright took the disks and sprinkled them across the universe via the complex web of intergalactic wormholes.

What happened next was the oddest thing anybody in attendance had ever seen, and you've just read what they'd been through in the previous unspecified time period! As Gorgol was an intergalactic being whose purpose was to unite the spheres, his presence inside a black hole caused some pretty weird things to occur. Here's your step-by-step guide to what happens when a servant of the Master enters a black hole:

**Step 1:** Anything currently inside the black hole, such as the floppy disks, get spat out of the other wormholes that are part of the complex system. This is so the black hole can really focus on what it has to do to its new inhabitant without getting distracted. As a result, the floppy disks were finally disseminated all over the universe.

**Step 2:** Atoms get a nice little stretch inside the black hole, and therefore the hero of the moment – Chuffles – was brought back to life! If you don't think that this is how physics works, ask yourself one thing – have you ever seen anybody get pulled into and subsequently chucked out of a black hole to a random planet elsewhere in the galaxy? No? Then who are you to say that this isn't how it works?! *Pipe down*, now Chuffles can go and live his high achieving life, far away from *S.S.R.R.P.P.*, maybe even ending up in middle management at Space-IBM. You want that for him, don't you?

**Step 3:** The body of the servant acts like a glue and binds all of the wormholes together, causing the rift in space to be closed, and for life to go back to normal.

'Wow!' exclaimed Martin S. Ronson, 'What a neatly finalised and rounded off story! I'm sure ready to live happily ever after!'

*Stronger than any armour*

# Space-Interlude II

The Master's eyes opened. The leek and potato space-soup was resting cold on the table.

The Master stood up.

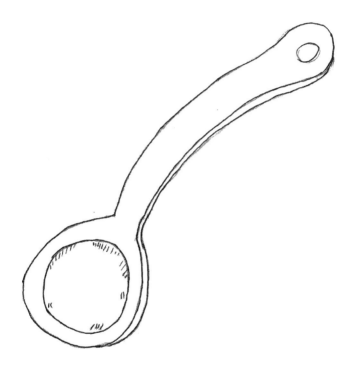

*Valaxion! (?)*

# 7-Teen

The clean-up was immense. There were thousands of bodies everywhere, and blood filled the themed streets of *S.S.R.R.P.P.* Bits of robot were all over the place, benches broken, bins overturned and children flattened. Bombs were still periodically exploding and fires ravaged the *Rainforest Café*, causing even more deforestation. Luckily there were over 80 casual members of staff still alive with all their required limbs to be able to put the clean-up into operation. They were happy for the extra hours.

The remaining basketball players were very pleased with themselves for being the inspiration for what they were calling *Space Jam II: Hoop the Loop,* the straight to DVD fully-animated sequel without Michael Jordan, Bill Murray or Wayne Knight. Stardew signed a few basketballs for them, after all she was still the daughter of the king, even though the king was dead as dead can be. Martin S. Ronson said goodbye to them, and we are pleased to say that he was never mistaken for a basketball ever again, except for in the bedroom at his own request.

The remaining diplomats decided, after a long debate and much diplomacy, that their summit was over. They attended the last few matches of the intergalactic basketball tournament to much enjoyment.

Following all these pleasantries our band of heroic heroes returned to *Chief Thunderous River's House of Spice*, took their seats, and munched down on some remaining naans that had survived the battle.

'Well I guess it's all over,' said Martin S. Ronson. 'The floppy disks have entered the black hole and there is no reason to think that they haven't been sent all over the galaxy to various inhabited planets. I very confident we've just saved life as we know it.' Amazingly there is no twist here, the floppy disks really had been sent all over the universe and, as Martin S. Ronson, our most comely and unlikely of heroes, spoke, individuals were picking up the disks and taking a look at the contents.

'I think you're right, pal,' said Biffin Bambright. 'I wouldn't want to be here with anyone except you guys, right here at the end of things. All A-okay. Now shall I take a look for some more of that fantastic curry we had earlier?'

Chuckling, Biffin got up and walked over to the back room pushing the two-way swinging door open a patch. He stopped dead in his tracks, and a single tear ran down the side and front of his great cylindrical alien face. In the heat of the battle and with the rush of constant adrenaline, the team had forgotten about one thing. Biffin opened the door wider so everyone else could peer in. On the shiny metal table lay the body of Mr Carmichael. He looked at peace, calm and collected, but in reality, he was just dead.

The whole group quickly burst into tears. The emotion

hit them like a space-fish to the face on a cold morning in Cumbria.

Stardew blubbed through her tears.

'Mr Carmichael! My friend!'

Phyllis was crying but had only really known Mr Carmichael for a short time. Regardless of this, death up close is a right tear jerker.

Biffin Bambright might have been crying too, but he was the one who had his shit together the most.

'We must give him a proper send off, a funeral fit for a princess' assistant. Stardew, where was Mr Carmichael from? What's his home planet?'

'Well, I guess that would be Leah-Cimrac out by the Tri-Star Nebula,' said Stardew, through sniffles.

'Right. Well I think it's time we left this dump of a theme park,' replied Mrs Bambright, his previous excitement towards *S.S.R.R.P.P.* thwarted by the war and the death.

'Let's bury Mr Carmichael in a coffin as grand as the man himself. I'll order one now.'

Everyone was pleased with this plan. Mr Carmichael deserved a good burial, and the plan gave them something to focus on rather than wallowing in the fact that none of them had a home, Stardew had no family, Biffin's shop was destroyed (by Stardew lest we forget), Phyllis was unprofessional and most of the public still disliked golplorx.

The group gathered together their bags while Phyllis and Martin S. Ronson went to pick up the space-limousine. As they walked through the theme park, past the desolation and the staff members' gentle mopping up of blood and robot-circuitry (staff members who had no idea of the psychological impact that this was having on their mental health), Martin S. Ronson was thinking about life. It was now or never, and our golplorx's little heart was beating worse than a bovine jockey at an equine rally *[Editor's note: what?]*.

'Phyllis?'

'Yes, Martin S. Ronson?' replied the beautiful jotaj.

'Now that this whole space-ordeal is coming to a neat and clean finish, how would you like to get to know each other a bit better, perhaps grab some yoffa some time?'

'I think that would be more than acceptable.' She leant over and gave him a little peck. He would have preferred a kiss, but pecking was fine. Wait, did we mention that Phyllis had a beak?

Around twenty to twenty-five minutes later the two pulled up, smiling, outside the curry house in Troy McClusky's limo.

The others had been busy and had fully assembled Mr Carmichael's coffin. It was quite the coffin. Biffin had ordered it on express delivery, which uses black holes for speedy arrival, but costs one hell of a lot of cold hard cash. The coffin was really sci-fi slick, silver and laser covered. It hovered by itself, with no need for carrying. Once again, the pallbearer is left behind in the wake of technology's unwavering progress.

Phyllis opened the back door of the space-limousine, and Mrs Bambright gave the floating casket, now housing the recently deceased Mr Carmichael, a light push. It floated elegantly through the open door and came to a rest just in front of the television. Biffin and Stardew got into the back of the limo with the coffin, while Phyllis and Martin S. Ronson sat in the front, so Phyllis could drive and Martin S. Ronson could keep her company.

As Phyllis began to pull away, an alien child ran out of the *House of Spice* and stepped in front of the car. Phyllis was a fantastic driver, so she was able to perform a *textbook* emergency stop before causing the young one any harm.

'Woah!' she shouted. 'That was a close one!'

'Indeed!' replied Martin S. Ronson. 'Thank god Mr Carmichael isn't driving!'

Nobody laughed. It was way too soon. Stardew burst into tears. Martin S. Ronson went bright red. Phyllis put her foot down, and our heroes got the heck out of the Tralmordian System!

A few minutes had passed, and nobody had said a word.

'Stardew,' asked Phyllis, 'do you know what sort of funeral Mr Carmichael would have liked? Was he space-religious at all? Did he tell you about any plans he had?'

'He told me exactly what kind of funeral he wanted one time, actually. It was pretty weird, we were just in the middle of watching an episode of *Mothers of Tsars Dance with the Stars Xtra Access: Behind the Tscenes* when he paused it and went into great detail. He went on for about fifteen minutes. I guess it's going to come in pretty... useful... now!'

The ellipses are meant to represent that she started crying, but I'm not sure how effectively they convey that. Anyway, she was crying now. Phyllis asked her another question.

'What did he tell you, Stardew?'

'He... said... that... he wanted... to be shot out of a cannon into the sea. He wasn't religious, but that's how every Carmichael before him had been laid to rest, and that's how he wanted to go out, too.'

Phyllis tapped on the Universal Positioning System and sighed.

'I'm sorry Stardew, but there's no way we're going to reach Leah-Cimrac in time, and the nearest planet with a body of water large enough to be classed as a sea is going to take us days to get to! If only we hadn't closed up that system of wormholes! What else can we do?'

'Oh he told me this too,' said Stardew, 'as I say, it was a weirdly long conversation. He said that if he couldn't be fired into the sea, then he'd like to be fired off into space. After all, he said, space is the sea of the sky.'

'That almost makes sense,' said Phyllis.

'Phyllis,' asked Stardew, 'is there a cannon shop nearby anywhere according to your Universal Positioning System?'

'Let me check.'

Phyllis checked.

'There isn't a shop, but there's a place where you can hire out cannons by the hour, and what's more, they even say they'll fire anything out into space for you!'

'Does that include dead bodies?'

'It literally says 'no exceptions'. We should head there now!'

So, that's what they did.

*Fit for a grand man*

# Chapter √324

The space-limousine touched down in the car park of this conveniently located cannon firing range. As he was no longer in the cold store area of the *House of Spice*, Mr Carmichael was beginning to smell, as one does after they have died.

'Hey, Mrs Bambright! You're not the smelliest anymore!' Martin S. Ronson shouted, in the second misjudged outburst of the last several paragraphs. He immediately regretted it, and saw the pangs of sorrow form on all of his friends' faces again. Apparently this was his way of dealing with grief, but it was going down worse than Roy 'Chubby' Brown would at the *Guardian* Christmas party, or conversely, a reading of the *Guardian* would at Roy 'Chubby' Brown's Christmas party.

Everybody got out of the limo, except Martin S. Ronson, who sat and took a deep breath. As everybody else stood and waited for him, he tapped the side of the coffin so it floated out of the door that it had come into.

They weren't expecting to see the sight that greeted them. A medium-sized queue of about fifteen groups snaked its way from the entrance of the cannon firing range and into the car park. Each of these groups also had a coffin floating alongside them, and they all looked as equally grief stricken.

'What on Diligord-4 is going on here?!' pondered Mrs

Bambright.

Stardew stepped forward to the group at the back of the line, and tapped a woman alien with frizzy blue hair and a metallic dress on the shoulder.

'Excuse me,' she said, 'who are all you people? What's going on here? We've come to send or beloved friend Mr Carmichael off into space as he wished, are you here to send your friend off into space as well?'

The frizzy haired alien nodded glumly.

'I am. Wanda Carmichael is inside that coffin. She was a great friend to all of us here. I am going to miss her greatly.'

Stardew gasped.

'Wanda Carmichael?! What are the chances of two Carmichaels dying on the same day, in the same area of space, with the same wish to be shot off into space if there isn't a sea close by?!'

'Two Carmichaels? I count fifteen,' said the blue-hair alien.

'Everybody here is a Carmichael?!'

'That's what this place is for! Whenever a Carmichael dies in this area, they are to be shot into space from these impressive cannons.' She gestured towards a row of cannons that were indeed impressive. They were covered in Latin.

'Just how many Carmichaels are out there?'

'I'm not sure, but Wanda said maybe a few million.

Their great-great-great grandparents had an incredibly large batch of offspring, as did all the generations that followed. Did Mr Carmichael here never attend the family gathering?'

Stardew's stomach dropped. Mr Carmichael had mentioned a few family reunions, but she'd always had something she needed him for on the day, and he never really pushed it. She wished she'd been a slightly more reasonable employer now.

'He didn't. I had no idea there were so many Carmichaels in the universe.'

'There's quite a few here today, unfortunately it's a busy shift for the cannon. A group of young Carmichael cousins had just started their dream job as rollercoaster technicians, and they were caught up the horrific events in the Tralmordian System today.'

'I'm so sorry,' replied Stardew.

'And to you. It is truly a dark day in the Carmichael family calendar.'

\*\*\*

Phyllis was waiting around, getting a bit impatient with this large queue of dead Carmichaels waiting for their chance to be shot out into space. As she stared about the room she read some of the posters on the walls. They were advertising many types of cannon. Space-cannons of course, but also antique artillery cannons from the 1840s, the trademark Xandeen Flash-Cannon 5000, Pachelbel's Canon in E# minor (this is a special key that can only be heard in Space, or if you play all of Terry Riley's body of work simultaneously) and even canon material officially accepted as part of the fictional universe. After learning much about types of cannon/canon, Phyllis decided to go to the toilet, and, like in any book, characters only go to the toilet when it has something to do with the story. She entered the stall and did her business. I'm not sure if you've ever seen a jotaj go to the toilet but it's quite the procedure. The suckers and tentacles get in the way no matter how you try it, and therefore there's a lot of hosing down needed at the end. You've probably noticed the hoses they have in intergalactic toilets and now you know what they are for.

Whilst still dripping from the hosing down, Phyllis spotted something on the floor of the stall. She reached down and picked it up. It was a floppy disk.

Still dripping, she trotted back into the shop.

'Hey guys, look what I've found! It's one of our floppy disks! One of those wormholes must have pooped it out here!'

The rest of her crew were all looking at the small flat screen TV on the wall. The news was on. Martin S. Ronson waved a hand at her in a *not now Phyllis* kind of way and pointed at the screen. She glanced up. There was a Blerghmanian news presenter on screen, and the headline read *Do Dynamic Dimensional Disks Declare Destiny?*

'Reports are coming in of hundreds upon thousands of floppy disks, an old outdated format of digital storage, having appeared seemingly out of nowhere on many planets across the galaxy. There has been much speculation as to the contents of these disks. It was not known whether they were dangerous or not. The latest from the *CHBMPD* (space-police) is that there is no danger to anyone who wants to track down a floppy disk-to-TrumpDrive™ converter, put a TrumpDrive™ in the TrumpDrive™ drive, and take a look at the contents.'

The tension in the room was massive. Martin S. Ronson was positively shaking. This was it, he had accomplished his task in this massive adventure, and all it took now was for the citizens of the galaxy to see what was on the disks. As long as enough people looked at the disks, news would spread and harmony would be restored to the galaxy. The news presenter continued.

'There is no danger on the floppy disks, instead there is...'

Everyone held their breath.

'...just disappointment. All the floppy disks contain is

this image of an old man's face.'

On the screen appeared a photo that was too close to home. At first the group thought it was poor ol' Mr Carmichael, but after a moment they could see the racism in his eyes, and realised that all they were looking at was a JPEG of Corey Carmichael's face. The Blerghmanian presenter continued.

'It has been decided that this floppy disk fiasco was simply a poor marketing scheme by a sad, rich, old comedian named Corey Carmichael. It is unknown why he decided to use floppy disks to advertise his comedy career, but it is known that Corey Carmichael has not been seen in public for the past few days.'

'What's happened?!' said Martin S. Ronson, his voice wavering as he spoke. 'That's not what was on the floppy disks. You saw it! YOU ALL SAW IT!' He was getting hysterical. Biffin grabbed him and said the most calming thing he could think of.

'Calm down, Martin S. Ronson!'

It worked. Martin S. Ronson started to take deep breaths and collect himself. Biffin then continued.

'I have a horrible feeling that when Corey copied all those floppy disks, he actually copied a JPEG of his face on to them. In which case, that's what has been sent all over the universe.'

Phyllis chipped in.

'So what you're saying is we're back to square one?'

'There's nothing square about it,' said Biffin, 'but yes, I guess we'll have to start this whole thing again and find another way to spread the word of the contents of the disk. Martin S. Ronson, buddy? Where's the original disk?'

'It's right here,' he said, pulling out a floppy disk from his special pocket, passing it to Mrs Bambright.

'Erm, this one says *From the desk of Corey Carmichael* on the back…'

He looked at Martin S. Ronson.

'Oh holy sweet mother of space-tits...'

*The things you find on the toilet floor*

# Space-Interlude: Third Time's the Charm

The soup was long cold, and the Master had finally had a proper shower, tired of all this washing in gold nonsense.

A group of followers trailed behind the Master as she walked slowly, yet purposefully, from one side of her massive spaceship to the other. This walk had taken over eighteen months. You may be wondering why the Master had been walking across her ship, seemingly doing nothing, whilst the rest of this story had been unfolding. Good question.

Unfortunately, whatever interdimensional travel she had gone through to get to this dimension from the black and dark and grim place (using another Spoon of Valaxion of course) had not had the same beautification effect that it had on Gorgol. She looked pretty much the same as the first interlude, just evil and masterful.

The ship had a crew of about seven-hundred thousand, which was required to keep all of its parts and processes running smoothly. The newest of these parts that required smooth running was a new, massive, orange laser.

The Master reached the control panel of the orange laser, which was located next to the state-of-the-art telescope, which was useful for looking at things which one might want to blow up.

'Have we checked this thing is working properly?' the Master asked. 'The last thing I want when we arrive is for the laser to fail when I'm trying to give those scoundrels who killed Gorgol what's coming to them.'

'We tried it yesterday!' replied a minor character, whose only line is this one.

'Yesterday,' retorted the Master, 'was yesterday. Today is today. A lot can happen in a day. A house can be torn down by a travelling collection of savages. A beloved servant can be crushed by a rollercoaster technician travelling at a great speed. And a laser can stop working. Let's have a go on it.'

The Master looked through the telescope to see if there was anything she could blow up. She looked around for a few seconds, and noticed another ship, which was roughly three-and-a-half times smaller than her ship but nonetheless also massive, a few hundred thousand kilometres away. She zoomed in and saw what seemed to be a worried looking jotaj with his left sucker all perked up. Disgusting. The jotaj was using the medical ward's waiting room for its intended purpose. He appeared to look straight back, although there is no way he would have been able to see the Master's ship from that distance without his own incredibly powerful telescope.

'That'll do,' said the Master.

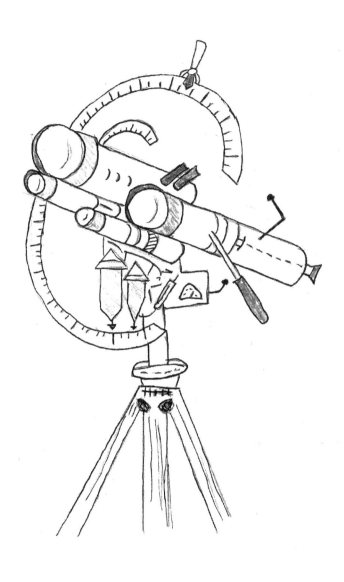

*You've got no (sc)hope of escaping this!*

# The Final Chapter

All our heroes were back in the parked space-limo. Biffin Bambright was rustling up some scrambled eggs on toast for Martin S. Ronson and the team. Don't ask what kind of eggs, you really don't want to know what kind of eggs they scramble in space.

Biffin carried the large tray through to the lounge area of the limo. Phyllis was kindly stroking Martin S. Ronson's back – he hadn't taken recent events well at all. He was snotting everywhere and wiping his nose with some kitchen towel, which is really not designed to be used on a supple golplorx nose like Martin S. Ronson's. Stardew handed him some toilet roll instead. This too is not great for wiping away snot, as it's literally designed to break up when wet. No one handed him a tissue. For goodness sake!

'Hey buddy! Don't despair, I've brought you some space eggs.'

Martin S. Ronson looked up at Mrs Bambright, his oldest friend (I think they've known each other a few days tops? But then again, Martin S. Ronson was part of a child golplorx army. So is he a few days old? He seems very mature. How long is a golplorx's lifespan? These are all good questions, but now is not the time to ask them) and said:

'*Eggs?!* You think I need *eggs* at a time like this?' He turned to look out the window, out at the vast emptiness of space, the endless void of cosmic intelligence and all that exists in the realm of matter. 'I'm not sure you understand. That floppy disk, and more importantly, its contents, were the single most important thing that could bring harmony to life in the galaxy. I believe I was led to that disk by fate.'

'Oh come on Martin S. Ronson,' replied Stardew sympathetically, 'you know there's no such thing as fate. We're in space for goodness sake!'

'Well not actually fate, it was just a figure of speech from the old country. But this whole ordeal with Gorgol and the rollercoasters and Mr Carmichael, in fact, all those bloody Carmichaels, has it all been for nothing?'

It was at this moment, while he was looking out of the window, that a massive, and this time we really mean massive, spaceship lifted into view. It was huge, and its orange laser had cooled down and was almost ready to be unleashed once more.

\*\*\*

On board the ship, the Master was watching the space-limo (formerly known at Troy McClusky's space-limo) and speaking to her battle commander, who was a great hulking beast of a creature. The kind of creature you can't imagine doing anything except grunting, being evil and killing things. If you think about it though, he must have some downtime now and again, just to recharge and get ready for the the next bit of evil and killing. I wonder what he does for leisure?

'Prepare the big orange laser, Commander. I want it pointing at that ship ready to blow as soon as I finish talking to this group of Gorgol-killers. He will be avenged!'

'Right you are ma'am,' the battle commander replied, his mind focussed on his new collection of fifties soul records that he planned to digitise tonight.

'What do you think of the speech? Does it convey how important Gorgol was, but also, lets them know that they've only mildly inconvenienced my plan to unite the spheres?' The Master had prepared an amazing speech which her commander had just proofread for her.

'Yes ma'am, fantastic speech ma'am'.

'Oh, trusted commander, you fill me with such self-esteem!'

The Master pushed a button, which caused a pneumatic shaft to get into gear, and slowly lower the door of the spaceship close to the ground. It landed with a thud next to the feet of Biffin Bambright, who had just come out of the limo, followed by his friend, the moping Martin S. Ronson.

'What the bloody hell is that?!' Biffin exclaimed, almost dropping his disgusting eggs onto the floor.

'I can barely see the other end of that ship!' shouted Stardew. 'That *has* to be the largest spaceship I've seen in my life! And I've seen some huge ones!'

The Master appeared in the doorway and let out a very evil laugh. It almost turned into a cackle, but she reigned it in with incredible skill.

'Why, thank you! I do pride myself on the incredible vastness of my vessel. Largest ship in the universe, by any measure. Feet or miles!'

'Who are you?!' shouted Stardew. 'Why is your massive ship here, at this cannon rental shop, where only people with the surname 'Carmichael' seem to get shot into space? Is that ship full of the other couple of million Carmichaels? Did they *all* die today?' She was saying this with sarcasm but it could have been true.

'I bring with me no dead Carmichaels. There are a few living ones in my massive crew though, there has to be, law of averages and all.'

'Well then why *are* you here?!'

'I could ask you the same question. Just why have you brought *your* deceased Carmichael to this cannon range?'

'As a matter of fact,' shouted Stardew, 'he just died *heroically* in battle! This is how he wanted to go out.'

'SILENCE!' shouted the Master.

'What do you mean silence? You asked me a quest–'

'–DOUBLE SILENCE! You have crossed me for the last time. My sweet Gorgol, the Uniter of Worlds, the Demon of the Magnetosphere and the Bringer of Soup was not only killed by your hand, but his body is now out of my grasp. He was a noble servant and you were not worthy to best him.'

Mrs Bambright spoke.

'Actually it wasn't us that killed Gorgol, it was this kid called Chuffles –'

'– TRIPLE SILENCE!' retorted the Master. 'Look at you all, what a group of lacklustre aliens. The feeble daughter of a dead king, who in his living days was just a pawn for my work. An ex-Bodyshop owner with a cylindrical head and a dirty, smelly, small golplorx with delusions about the future and life and destiny who just happened by a floppy disk one day, and took that to mean he was part of something bigger, rather than just a smudge on the sole of my interdimensional shoe. Useless, all of you.'

Martin S. Ronson had noticed something at this point, and we certainly hope you did too. Who was missing? The answer? Phyllis. Martin S. Ronson glanced around the room and noticed the unmistakable sight of one of Phyllis' leg tentacles disappearing around a corner. She had something up her sleeve and it wasn't yoffa, that's for sure. There was only one thing Martin S. Ronson had to do, and that was figuratively buy as much time for Phyllis as he literally could. Luckily for him, them and us, the Master was ready to unleash her epic speech to the group. Her speech was long, insulting and interesting. It went into great detail about the uniting of the spheres, Gorgol's childhood, the origin of the floppy disk and the importance of its contents for the galaxy and exactly why she was evil and wanted to destroy everything.

\*\*\*

Also luckily for us, Phyllis had got out while she could. She snuck behind everyone and managed to get on the big pneumatic ramp that the Master had used to descend on to the space-limo. She ran up the ramp with her tentacles (this will be really cool to watch in the feature film, there's a lot of 360 degree action going on so you won't regret the purchase of two pairs of single use 3D glasses) and entered the vastness of the really big spaceship.

Being very sneakful and careful at the same time, she crawled on her belly past the reception desk at the entrance of the ship. The lazy receptionist had been idly looking up the history of the Tralmordian Royal Family on Wikipedia (not the same royal family as Stardew's though, as you are well aware), and probably wouldn't have noticed her anyway, but Phyllis didn't want to take that risk. She very slowly crawled behind the receptionist and then in one swift movement wrapped her strongest tentacle around his neck and choked him until he dropped to the floor. She hastily undressed him and put on his uniform, a simple black alien-jacket and a black flat-cap as well as a name tag that said *Phionwrack*. She whispered *'Jackpot'* to herself at this point, as it's a unisex name.

'Now,' she said to herself in the way that real people don't. 'Where the hell do I go?'

From the reception area there were long corridors pointing in many directions. Phyllis took a moment to inspect the signage and saw that the Command Centre was only 50 miles away, effectively a centimetre in the hugeness of this ship. She thought this would be a good place to head to. Contrary to Martin S. Ronson's belief, Phyllis didn't have a plan, but just like a lot of adventurers (and authors) she hoped something would come to her on the way.

She started to head down the corridor towards the Command Centre and jumped on to one of the staff only bicycles, breaking the very first rule of the bikes. The Master was a very good employer and encouraged exercise, health and wellbeing at every possibility. Workers used to use segways to get around, but the new health scheme replaced them all with bicycles, which left the staff a bit disgruntled, but all the more healthy. The few members of staff who couldn't ride a bike were swiftly fired.

Phyllis rode the bike about 100 metres before the corridor joined a moving travelator. She kept on cycling, and eventually this travelator joined on to a bigger one. Phyllis glanced over the edge and became witness to the greater operation of the Master's workforce. Below her were hundreds and hundreds of travelators, all criss-crossing in a crazy space-spaghetti junction of order and engineering. Cycling bikes on all of these travelators were thousands of the Master's employees, all going about their daily duties.

Some were heading to the janitor's store room to collect the essential equipment to clean up after the recent meeting of the deadly Wrozzle-Worm Arts Collective. Others were returning from various war-rooms where they orchestrate wars in other dimensions, discovering the best tactics before they are put to practice in this dimension. Even more aliens were management consultants. There were loads of management consultants, even though they're of no value in space, much like on Earth.

There were of course about 800 members of staff who had been cycling on the travelators with a look of purpose on their face, day-in day-out for about six years, simply waiting for the end of the day and eventually the end of their working life when their pension would kick in, by which time they would be happy to retire and live out their golden years as part of an ex-pat community, with well toned legs and a sore bum.

Phyllis followed the many signposts along the way leading her directly to the Command Centre. Once she reached the end of the line she hopped off her bike, which instantly disintegrated in order to be reintegrated back where she found it ready for the next rider.

As Phyllis turned the corner to the Command Centre, she saw a huge room of people waiting around with bits of paper in their hands. With true belief and faith in her disguise, she decided to speak to one of the waiters (staff members who were waiting, not people who serve customers in restaurants).

'Err, hello there, fellow member of this excellently vast ship, pray do tell, what is the meaning of this large group of staff members? Ist thou in a meeting of sorts?' Phyllis had no idea why she was talking like this, but the pressure was starting to get to her. The other member of staff turned to Phyllis.

'Why are you talking like that Phionwrack?' He noted the name tag as he spoke.

'Ermm, oh, don't worry about that. Could you tell me what's going on with all these people waiting around?'

'Well, clearly you've never had any problems with your

pension. We're waiting to see the Commander, the Master's right-hand alien. Since the Pension Department was merged with the Big Orange Laser Department, the waiting time for pension queries has more than quadrupled. He simply doesn't have the time, and to be honest I don't blame him. If I had a massive laser to point at things for the Master to blow up in her never-ending quest for dominance over the galactic spheres and the contents of obsolete data storage formats, then I would never be hanging around answering dull pension queries.'

'Big Orange Laser Team?' asked Phyllis.

'Yes… you know… the Big Orange Laser that we use to blow up our enemies? It's pointed at those scoundrels outside right now. How do you not know about the Big Orange Laser? This is arousing suspicion inside me.'

Phyllis gulped.

'Of course I know about the Big Orange Laser!' she lied. 'I thought it was operated by whole team of aliens, not just one!'

'Ah!' replied the suspicious staff member. 'Common mistake! There is a team of aliens, although only one is on shift at a time. Poor management if you ask me, look how long this line is! That's management consultants for you. It's just the Commander in there right now, sorting out the pensions and laser operation.'

'Right. Well how do I get in line, and how long do you reckon it will take me to get an audience with the Commander?' asked Phyllis.

'Well I've been here just over three weeks and I'm number 487 in the queue, so you do the maths.' Phyllis didn't do any maths, but assumed it would be a long time. 'In order to join the queue you have to go up to that little machine on the wall and press the red button to get a ticket. There's a queue for the machine but it only takes a few minutes, the machine is very efficient. We all hope and pray that it won't be merged with another department any time soon.'

'Right,' said Phyllis, who was actually thinking *fuck that*. Don't forget that she'd worked as a spy for Histapine Horticultural Husbandry corporation for many years, and everyone knows what a blessed jewel of human resources that place is. No, she would not dare to stoop to wait a ridiculously long time (we haven't done the maths either) to speak to the Commander in order to do something to stop the Master. She was starting to think of a plan involving this Big Orange Laser but didn't have all of the details worked out yet. She had no idea how long the Master's speech was but she doubted it would be that long.

\*\*\*

The Master was about forty-five minutes into her villainous speech, and everybody was starting to achieve perfect clarity about what exactly all of this floppy disk, sphere unity and Spoon of Valaxion business was all about. She was now taking questions.

'One second,' shouted Biffin Bambright, who'd had his hand up for a little while, 'so the Spoon of Valaxion isn't a real spoon at all?!'

'Ah, good question!' replied the Master, who really enjoyed giving thorough explanations to those she was about to destroy. She had watched a lot of James Bond films growing up, and enjoyed the part where the Bond villain would explain their plan in detail to the perverted, alcoholic scoundrel. She would always turn off the space-video player just before the speech was somehow interrupted in a manner that saved 007 and caused the villain a great misfortune.

'Ah, good question!' she'd already said, but I thought I'd repeat it as I went off on a tangent. 'So, there is no single physical spoon that is the Spoon of Valaxion any more, but I can nominate any spoon that I wish to hold that title. As long as there is a nominated spoon, all of the complicated maths that I just explained holds up.'

'That makes perfect sense.' replied Biffin.

'Any more questions?' asked the Master.

Martin S. Ronson was quaking in his little figurative boots. He knew Phyllis would be working on something, but she needed more time!

'Wait!' he shouted. 'What were you saying about the equilibrium of the second sphere? Without the presence of the nominated spoon then the sphere would collapse under the weight of its own gravity?'

Stardew groaned.

'Have you not been paying attention?' said Stardew, who was getting restless and hadn't noticed the lack of Phyllis or thought about how she might be doing something to save the day.

'Sorry!' he shouted. 'I could use use a quick recap!'

'As you wish!' shouted the Master. 'Let me go into even greater detail this time, lest anyone leaves this existence uninformed!

***

Phyllis had taken a ticket anyway, which had given her a plausible reason to be hanging around the doorway of the Pension and Big Orange Laser Department. She'd formulated the plan now. It wasn't particularly sophisticated. She was a beautiful woman, as you have seen. She was going to go into the room, distract the commander with her suckers and then take control of the Big Orange Laser and shoot the Master in her evil head. She hated that she was stooping to using dated, gender driven plot lines, but was a little bit drunk off the WKD and was struggling to think of anything else.

She pushed just ahead of the person at the front of the queue, and knocked firmly on the door. Nobody answered, obviously, they were incredibly busy. She knocked again, and before she could await a response, she pushed the door open. Naturally, everyone behind her was a bit miffed at her pushing in but they didn't do anything about it. They were too polite.

She entered the room with both suckers raised high above her head, and sang her seduction song, which was *I Like to Move it* by the outfit Reel to Reel. The Commander didn't have time to reply before he was enchanted by her beauty and quality taste in music.

'Hi there,' smouldered Phyllis.

'Hi,' replied the commander, who had actually met Phyllis at drama club fifteen years previously, but neither of them could remember that.

'What a lovely, Big, Orange Laser you have there. Mind if I take a look?' She slinked over to the button and rested her hand over the top. This was one power play too far. The Commander snapped out of it.

'You need to step away from the button, ma'am. I don't care how silky your suckers are. You need to get out of here right now. Unless of course you have some kind of pension query and a qualifying numbered ticket for me, in which case I'm happy to help. If not, you'd better like to move it, move it towards that door.'

'You're gonna have to make me.'

She lifted her arm above the button to fire the laser, in a very purposeful manner. This angered the commander.

'You have NO idea what you are messing with there! Do you want to jeopardise this whole mission?'

'Oh, darling,' said Phyllis, 'that's exactly what I want.' This made the Commander's blood boil. Phyllis had no plans to hit that button yet, for she had no idea where it was pointed. She had no idea if it would annihilate her friends, or kill the Master and end this sorry tale. But she'd overplayed her hand.

The commander lunged at her.

Phyllis dodged to her right.

The commander fell with full force into the button.

The Big Orange Laser fired.

\*\*\*

'Okay,' said Martin S. Ronson, a minute or so previously.

'So there are no ducks on Diligord-5?'

'No!' shouted the Master, who was losing her patience. 'How did we even get onto this topic?!'

'I think it was something to do with Gorgol's favourite childhood meals?' replied Biffin Bambright. He was really bored, and hoped that they'd either defeat the Master or be killed soon.

'Right! I have had enough of this!'

The Master had had enough of this.

'I have a Big Orange Laser ready to blow all of you treacherous beings and your dead Carmichaels to smithereens! The laser should now be warmed up! I'm going to get back on my ship and float off to a safe distance before it's engaged!'

'Well, actually only one of the Carmichaels belongs to us,' said Martin S. Ronson.

'For goodness sake!' replied the Master, 'your time is up!'

Stardew had been quiet for a while.

'Now!' she shouted.

The Master turned around, confused. Stardew was on her hands and knees, perpendicularly behind her.

'What on earth are you doing?!' she enquired, with vigour.

'NOW!' Stardew screamed again.

The Master turned around to see a large, cylindrical head barging towards her. This large, cylindrical head hit her square in the chest, and she tripped backwards, over the primed back of the daughter of the king.

'Woahh!' she blurted on her way down, and a bit of spit flew out of her mouth. She landed with a thud on the floor. She stayed on her back and fully cackled, despite avoiding cackling so well earlier on.

'You fools! You think that's enough to defeat me?! I am the most powerful being in the universe! I will DESTROY...'

\*\*\*

Inside the ship, Phyllis had just moved to the right. A Big Orange Laser was fired. Right into the head of the all powerful, all seeing, all knowing Master.

If anybody else had been hit by the laser, they would have been immediately evaporated along with whatever planet lay behind them. Fortunately for everybody currently visiting the space cannon place, the Master was different. She absorbed the full force of the Big Orange Laser right in the centre of her interdimensional soul, but even she was no match for its Bigness and Orangeness.

It was a sight to behold. She turned bright orange, then

to black, and then imploded in on herself. She shrank, and she shrank, until she became a small neutron star, half the size of Martin S. Ronson. He had just acquired a golf club that he was going to use as part of a plan of his own (that he'd thankfully not to put into action as it was a terrible plan that would have killed them all), but he was able to utilise the five iron now. He pitched up next to the star formerly known at the Master, and drove her right off into space.

'FORE!' he shouted. Golf wasn't very popular in space for obvious reasons, so nobody got why he said this.

'That was a real stroke of good luck,' said Stardew, only talking about the fact that the laser fired in exactly the right place at the right time, unaware that this could also be a terrible golf pun.

Gorgol was dead. His master was dead. Her crew were no longer under her spell. Yes, she had been a decent employer (the Pension and Big Orange Laser Department merger wasn't her idea), but the 70,000 crew members could now see that she was a real menace to society, and they'd been aiding its downfall. When Mark Zuckerberg is fed to the artificially intelligent race of wolves that he has been testing in developing countries under the guise of an open internet for all, the software engineering team at Facebook are going to have a similar epiphany.

'Ladies and gentlemen,' spoke Martin S. Ronson, softly.

'I believe we were gathered here to say goodbye to our dear friend.' Our heroes nodded simultaneously.

### A short time later...

Seven hundred thousand newly unemployed people lined the windows of the biggest space-ship that you or I had ever seen, with their feet together and a salute at the end of their arms. Trumpets were playing the Carmichael family anthem.

Biffin Bambright, Stardew, Phyllis, and Martin S. Ronson, each wearing their new medal, stood next to a long line of cannons. One by one, a space coffin fit for a Carmichael, and each containing one, was pushed inside. When each cannon was primed, Martin S. Ronson turned to the control room and gave a thumbs up to the cannon operator. Possibly not the most efficient way to do it, but definitely the most emotive.

It was a sight to behold. There was the loudest explosion any of them had heard since the Big Orange Laser was fired a few minutes previously and probably damaged their hearing quite badly. A crescent of Carmichael coffins flew across the sky, like a dancing arrangement of beautiful birds first thing on a spring morning. Martin S. Ronson thought of his old friend, and wiped a tear from his eye.

He had made up his mind. Gorgol and the Master were dead. The universe could be at peace. He was going to live life to the full. He was going to marry Phyllis, the love of his life. He was going to remain good friends with Biffin Bambright and see Stardew occasionally. He was going to live a good life, just as Mr Carmichael would have wanted him to.

And he was going to forget about that blasted floppy disk.

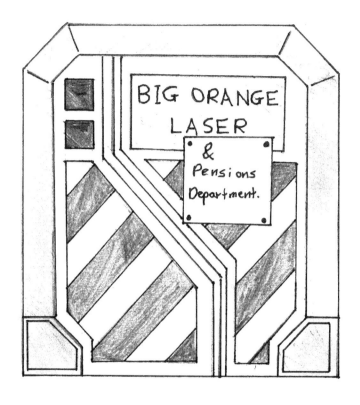

*A ridiculous merger*

# Epilogue

**Klechyms-16: The Zroev'ynsy System**
**Sometime around Chapter 16**

It was a warm sunny day (86 degrees centigrade and/or fahrenheit depending on the planet's temperature systems) and the moon was orbiting its host at the right moment to make it visible from the surface. Across the fields of his farm, Gnach had been toiling a hard days toil, and it was about time for him to return to his seven wives, four husbands and sixteen children. It was a hard life in space, and the recent economic climate had not been good to Gnach. The destruction of Diligord-4, 16.358 lightyears ($9.616255 \times 10^{13}$ miles) away had resulted in a crash in the price of muepseo grain, his prime produce, and Gnach had decided to turn to breeding fluffy-alhimi in a drastic attempt to sell their meat and shoes to anyone who would buy. He'd never bred fluffy-alhimi before, and it was taking a while for him to get to grips with their interesting feeding habits and the best way to get rid of his old yoffa roots, which are deadly to their immune system. He hadn't even fully planned how he would deal with the sacrificial life force necessary for two fluffy-alhimi to mate, however he had noted that he had sixteen useless children.

With his fork hanging over his supple alien shoulder, he began trudging back home. Each step was long and laborious. Gnach's mind was racing. How was he going to feed his family like this? For the last few weeks they'd been eating out of tins of fleshy beans, which would eventually give his children ricketts and his wives scurvy.

The farmer was just about coming to some kind of business strategy that genuinely would save his farm (it involved renting out his barns to travelling ramblers), but he very quickly forgot all about this, as across the field he spotted a pillarprick of light (like a pinprick, but able to be spotted from a further distance). This was a very curious thing to be seen on Gnach's Farm. The agricultural worker decided to walk over to the beam of light. By the time he got there it was slightly wider and between the wisps of photons and dust, for a split second, he thought he could see a fat cylindrically-headed creature in a purple leotard, and a massive ballista. He quickly attributed this to exhaustion, deciding he'd better carry on home to get his full eight hours before the next day of hard work (he really resented the rest of his family for putting in no work on the farm). Just as he started to walk something hit him on the back of the head and bounced to the ground in front of him. Gnach looked down, bent over, and picked up the object.

It was a floppy disk.

He was going to disregard this as space trash, but something bigger kept his interest. Unbeknownst to Gnach, this floppy had no JPEGs of Corey Carmichael's face on it. No, it contained much, much more.

*Gnach – one lucky farmer*

# Twopilogue

**Pouxxehx: The Tyr'ikx system**
**Also sometime around chapter sixteen**

SLAM! WHAM! BAM! Chuffles smacked the floor with a wallop. Half a space-second later the deceased body of Gorgol landed right on top of him.

'Eugh,' said Chuffles, who rolled the corpse of the flipping ugly gargoyley demon thing off of him.

He got to his knees and then his feet. Now that he was standing normally he looked around. Where the space was he?

The last thing Chuffles could remember was shouting to his one true beloved, Phyllis the jotaj, telling her that he would never let her down and that he loved her excellent suckers. He knew now, he just had a feeling, that he was very, very far from *Screaming Sam's Rickety Rocking Party Park*. He was, in fact, 43.54 light years (13.34 parsecs) from the Tralmordian System and his place of work. Commuting was going to be hell.

The reality of the situation began to dawn on the young

rollercoaster attendant and he started to cry. His mother was going to wonder where he was when he didn't come home tonight, and she'd probably be worried eventually. He sniffed and spluttered. Strangely, his tears lifted off his weird alien cheeks into the air and dissolved gently, dispersing out in the wind. Chuffles continued to sob.

A nearby qlukom jerked its vicious head upwards, sniffed twice, and smelt the salty taste of teenage tears. It pegged it toward the source of the tears, unfurling its ring of teeth, all of which were lined with another ring of teeth.

Chuffles wiped his nose on his *S.S.R.R.P.P.* uniform sleeve and let out of a big sigh/groan/howl. A vibration in the ground alerted him to something happening in the vicinity. Looking upward, he saw a figure driving towards him at great speed. It was obvious that this wasn't anything good, and he gave a feeble attempt at running away from whatever it was. Unfortunately for Chuffles, qlukoms are pretty darn fast and it reached him shortly after his futile attempt at a getaway.

The many teeth of the qlukom ripped into the fleshy skin of his belly and his entrails were released, the putrid gas and the half digested food falling out. Green blood was flowing freely as Chuffles was flung into the air. By the time he reached the ground it was unclear whether he had just passed out from the pain or was already dead. What is for sure is that he never did work in middle-management at space-IBM.

*Almost as scary as a career at space-IBM*

# Threepilogue: the Final Epilogue

## The Phyllis-Ronson Household
## The Future

It was Wednesday evening, and Martin S. Ronson was hunched over his laptop once more, trawling space-eBay for bargains, with terrible posture. His long, dirty beard was itching again. He hadn't washed in months, not even in gold, of which he had none.

Phyllis was long gone and the two hadn't spoken for a fair while. Stardew had been in prison for the last six years after eventually being caught, tried and sentenced for the obliteration of an entire planet and the death of 400 billion.

He bit off some yoffa from his concentrated yoffa bar and let the crumbs (and the juice) fall to the floor, and all over the crotch of his jeans. The carpet was covered in bits of yoffa from all the previous times he'd done this, and all of his unwashed jeans had suffered the same fate.

He stared at the results for his space-eBay search. It was the same search that he had performed every morning, noon and night for the last five years:

*FLOPPY DISK*

He looked at the results. There were thousands. No matter how many he bought, more and more made their way onto space's premier online auction site. He sighed, deeply.

A few years previously he'd spent his time riding around the galaxy visiting as many charity shops as he could, buying all their floppy disks to the great delight of the till staff. He'd told Phyllis he'd been on business with work, but then the debt letters started rolling in (electronically). She'd left him, and then the yoffa habit had begun.

Mrs Bambright (who had opened a new, successful Bodyshop on Diligord-5) had tried his best to console the golplorx, but it hadn't really worked, and the well of despair had sucked Martin S. Ronson in. The number of times he'd loaded a floppy disk and seen Corey Carmichael's face appear was astonishing. He'd also found loads of information on businesses from the 80s that really should have been destroyed responsibly.

Today was different though, he was feeling more low than he ever had before, and for the first time in a while he knew deep in his heart that what he had been searching for was out of his grasp.

He hadn't bought any floppy disks on space-eBay for the last few days, but this morning a package from the website had arrived. It didn't contain any obsolete storage though. It contained a blender.

Martin S. Ronson opened the package and spent the next half hour putting his new blender together and plugging it into the mains. He pushed the main blending button, and heard its sharp, unforgiving blades whirr. He sighed again, more deeply.

He put the blender on the floor, just next to his desk. He threaded a piece of string through a small metal loop that he had attached to the desk. The string had a weight on one end, and a counterweight on the other. The weight was just about heavy enough to press the blending button on a brand new blender if it was dropped from a great enough height.

He then continued to place many different objects in a beautiful setup, creating an eclectic Rube Goldberg machine. After forty-six minutes, and no lifting of spirits, Martin S. Ronson blew on a pinwheel, starting the machine in motion. He climbed into the blender and stared out of the window of his house into the vastness of space, the source of all his troubles.

After about two minutes of Rube Goldberging, the lid of the blender snapped shut. The point of no return.

A buzz sounded. The Rube Goldberg machine carried on relentlessly. Martin S. Ronson rotated in the blender. He had left his flip phone open on the side. A text.

He squeezed up against the glass of the blender and squinted to see what it was. The text was from Biffin Bambright.

*I've found it.*

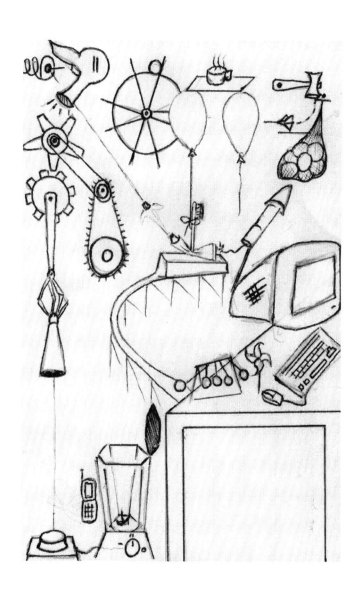

*All good things*

# Acknowledgements

**James Cressey**

I would like to thank Tom for
writing this book with me.

**Tom Williams**

I would like to thank James for
writing this book with me.

**Callum Winter**

I would like to thank Tom and James for asking me to
draw some pictures.

# About the Authors

## Tom Williams

Tom Williams rented a pedalo on the Norfolk Broads in 2007 and left his bag in the locker at his own risk. It was this risk that led him to writing once more. He lives alone in the marshes, you've probably seen him around. In 2001, Tom Williams was awarded the prize for Best General Friction but the static got to him and he never claimed the award. Tom has been referring to breakfast as 'petit dejeuner' for the last three weeks and it doesn't look like he's going to stop any time soon. He did get his bag back without a hitch.

## James Cressey

James Cressey is the definition of an underdog. Always picked last at his all American high school during gym class, he learned at an early age that he'd have to pull up his white socks with the red-and-blue trim and work hard to impress his peers. Is this his final act, the part where it looks like the team full of testosterone-fuelled athletes are going to win the championship and take the trophy home to their pushy fathers, but in a twist of unparalleled courage he claims the glory for his own? You'd better read this book and find out. Unless you have just read it, then you know the answer to that question.

This page intentionally left blank

32656423R00188

Printed in Poland
by Amazon Fulfillment
Poland Sp. z o.o., Wrocław